LEAD VENDETTA

Billy Swill snarled and reached for his sixgun. He wasn't slow, but he wasn't nearly fast enough, either. Fargo had his gun out before Billy could clear leather, and he fired once from the hip. The slug spun Billy around and sent his revolver flying.

For a moment the Swills were frozen. Then Clancy spun on Fargo, fury turning him reckless. "You shot my brother, you son of a—"

"I can do the same to the rest of you," Fargo said, sliding his Colt into his holster, brazenly inviting them to try.

Instead, Clancy motioned for his brothers to get out the door. As they filed out, Clancy gave Fargo a look that would wither a cactus. "I don't care how famous you are. You just made the biggest mistake of your life. No one puts lead into a Swill and lives to brag about it." He slowly backed out. "The newspapers will have a story to print, sure enough. But the headline will read: 'Trailsman Dies in Seven Devils Country!'"

THE
TRAILSMAN
#247

SEVEN
DEVILS
SLAUGHTER

by

Jon Sharpe

Ⓢ

A SIGNET BOOK

SIGNET
Published by New American Library, a division of
Penguin Putnam Inc., 375 Hudson Street,
New York, New York 10014, U.S.A.
Penguin Books Ltd, 80 Strand,
London WC2R 0RL, England
Penguin Books Australia Ltd, Ringwood,
Victoria, Australia
Penguin Books Canada Ltd, 10 Alcorn Avenue,
Toronto, Ontario, Canada M4V 3B2
Penguin Books (N.Z.) Ltd, 182–190 Wairau Road,
Auckland 10, New Zealand

Penguin Books Ltd, Registered Offices:
Harmondsworth, Middlesex, England

First published by Signet, an imprint of New American Library,
a division of Penguin Putnam Inc.

First Printing, May 2002
10 9 8 7 6 5 4 3 2 1

The Trailsman

Beginnings . . . they bend the tree and they mark the man. Skye Fargo was born when he was eighteen. Terror was his midwife, vengeance his first cry. Killing spawned Skye Fargo, ruthless, cold-blooded murder. Out of the acrid smoke of gunpowder still hanging in the air, he rose, cried out a promise never forgotten.

The Trailsman they began to call him all across the West: searcher, scout, hunter, the man who could see where others only looked, his skills for hire but not his soul, the man who lived each day to the fullest, yet trailed each tomorrow. Skye Fargo, the Trailsman, the seeker who could take the wildness of a land and the wanting of a woman and make them his own.

Seven Devils country, 1861—
Evil comes in human guise, snaring the innocent
deep among the silent, dark hills.

1

Skye Fargo liked to play poker as much as the next man. He liked the challenge, the thrill of pitting his wits against others in a high-stakes contest. But one thing he didn't like was a cardsharp. Tinhorns who cheated rather than play fair. Men who thought they were as slick as axle grease and went about fleecing tenderfeet and wide-eyed fools.

Fargo was no greenhorn, and he sure as hell was no fool. He was a big, broad-shouldered man with piercing lake-blue eyes and the muscular grace of a mountain lion in the way he moved and held himself. He favored buckskins and boots and a red bandanna, and strapped around his lean waist was a Colt, its grips worn smooth from regular use. Now, as he stared across the table at the polecat who was cheating, his blue eyes lit with an inner fire no one else noticed. He kept a poker face as he watched the man rake in the pot, then slid his cards toward the dealer.

"Yes, sir," the card cheat crowed, his porcine face aglow with greed. "Lady Luck has been sitting in my lap this whole game."

"And here I thought you were pregnant," quipped a player to Fargo's left. He was tall and lean and wore a black frock coat, a white shirt, and a black hat tilted low over his dark eyes. Unless Fargo missed his guess, the tall drink of water was a professional gambler, and like him, had spotted the heavyset cardsharp's sleight of hand.

The cheat glanced down at his ample belly and frowned. "I don't much like having folks poke fun at my expense, Denton." His clothes were as slovenly as he was, and consisted of a cheap suit, a bowler smeared with grime, and a shirt that served as a catchall for food that missed his mouth. But there was nothing cheap about the Smith and Wesson buckled to his left hip.

The gambler smiled thinly and responded, "I don't much care what you like, Mr. Swill. And I'll thank you not to use that tone with me ever again." As he spoke, he rested his right arm on the table.

Fargo heard the scrape of metal on wood. It was obvious that the gambler had a derringer up his sleeve. Swill realized it, too. He flushed with resentment but didn't say anything more.

"Gentlemen, gentlemen, please!" declared the dealer. His name was Harry Barnes and he owned the ramshackle excuse for a saloon. The only watering hole in the small settlement of Les Bois, it boasted a plank counter for a bar, four tables that needed new legs, and chairs that creaked when those seated in them so much as twitched. "This is supposed to be a friendly game. Let's not have any trouble."

"Fine by me," Swill said.

The last two players, both locals, bobbed their heads in agreement, and one of them cast a sly look at Swill.

Only then did Fargo catch on that the game itself was rigged. Swill wasn't playing alone. The card mechanic had partners. Among the gambling fraternity, it was known as a card mob. Fargo had a hunch all three local men were in on it. Not Barnes, though. The owner played too ineptly. A friendly old cuss who had opened the saloon as much to satisfy his own craving for liquor as anything else, he was also a chatterbox.

Barnes began gathering in the rest of the cards. A half-empty bottle of rotgut was perched next to his elbow, and every so often he would take a healthy swig. Now, pausing, he lifted the bottle to his mouth, gulped a few times, smacked his grizzled lips, and sighed with contentment. "I sure am glad you boys happened by," he said to Fargo and the gambler. "Other than an occasional wagon train off the Oregon Trail, we don't see all that many new faces here."

Fargo could see why. Les Bois was well off the beaten path. Founded by a French-Canadian trapper who gave the place its name, the settlement was situated near the Boise River. It was literally in the middle of nowhere, miles north and east of the Oregon Trail. Even calling it a settlement was giving it more credit than was due. It consisted of the saloon, a stable, and a sorry excuse for a general store. That was all. There were no homes, no families. Not in town, at any rate. Most of the locals were backwoods sorts. Hunters and trappers, men who lived off the land. Recluses who shunned human company. Outcasts who wanted nothing to do with civilization or its trappings; unsavory types like Swill and his partners, who weren't above trying to fleece a couple of travelers.

Fargo sat back and took a sip of whiskey. He was on his second glass and his gut was pleasantly warm. And empty. He had been on the go most of the day and stopped over in Les Bois on a whim. Soon the sun would set and he would have to find a spot to bed down for the night. Tomorrow he would move on, bound for the Pacific Coast.

Barnes began dealing. The deck was in front of him, and he slipped the cards off the top slowly, one-by-one, exaggerating his movements so no one could accuse him of anything shady. Glancing at Fargo, he remarked, "You haven't mentioned your name yet, friend."

"Are you sure?"

Barnes blinked, then chortled. "I get it. That's your way of telling me to mind my own business." He slid a card across. "I'm not trying to be nosy, mister. I just see no reason to sit here like a bunch of tree stumps."

Swill made a sniffing sound. "Hell, Harry, you prattle like a woman at times. I swear, it's enough to drive a gent to drink." He guffawed loudly and was joined by the other two locals.

Harry Barnes stiffened, then said something peculiar.

"You would know all about women, wouldn't you, Gus?"

To Fargo's surprise, the cheat came half out of his chair and his left hand dropped to his Smith and Wesson.

Swill's jowls worked and his cheeks puffed out like those of a riled squirrel. For a few seconds it appeared he would draw, but instead he merely glowered and eased back down. "You ought to keep a rein on that tongue of yours, Harry. It'll be the death of you one day if you're not mighty careful."

The other two locals were also glaring. Barnes shriveled under their gaze, then forced a grin and tried to lighten the mood by saying, "You know me, boys. Always gabbing away. No one ever takes me seriously."

"You'd best hope to God they don't," Swill said.

Fargo's curiosity was aroused. The saloon owner's comment hardly merited such hostility. "There must be a shortage of women in these parts," he mentioned to see how they'd react.

Swill and the others clammed up. Swill pretended to be interested in his filthy fingernails and the other two just stared at the table.

Only Barnes responded. "Ain't that the truth, friend. Most feminine critters don't cotton to living in the wilds. They like a nice home and pretty dresses and all that foofaraw. Not a one-room cabin off in the sticks." He nodded toward the bar. "Mabel, there, is fixing to move on to San Francisco just as soon as she saves up a couple of hundred dollars."

"Which shouldn't take her more than five or ten years," Swill threw in, and he and his friend chortled.

Mabel was the sole female inhabitant of Les Bois. In her late twenties, she had red hair that she wasn't fussy about keeping brushed and had a pretty face on which she dabbed more war paint than ten Sioux warriors combined. She wore a tight red dress that clung to her like a second layer of skin. A couple of minutes ago she had strayed over to the bar to refill her glass. She heard Swill's comment, and as she sashayed back she said, "What do you know, you dunderhead? One more year

4

in this flea-ridden dive should do it." She halted beside Fargo's chair and brushed his shoulder with her painted nails. "What about you, handsome? Care to treat a lady to a few drinks later?"

Fargo was the last man in the world to ever refuse female company. "See me later," he said. At the moment he couldn't afford to be distracted from the game.

The cards had been dealt. Everyone was contemplating their hands. Fargo had two kings, a queen, a seven, and a three. Swill opened, indicating he had a pair or better. Fargo stayed in, and when his turn came to ask for more cards, he requested two. He held onto the queen on the chance he might get another. He didn't, but he did receive another king and a four of clubs.

Swill had a good hand, too—or so he tried to convince everyone by raising the stakes. Barnes and the other locals bowed out.

Fargo stayed in.

"That's ten dollars to you, friend," Swill said to the gambler. "Unless you'd rather be smart and get out while you still have a shirt on your back."

Denton's thin lips curled in contempt. "I reckon I'll keep playing, Mr. Swill. I aim to see this through to the end."

"Your choice," Swill said, shrugging. And as he shrugged, he slid one of his cards up his right sleeve and replaced it with a card from up under his left. He was quick, Fargo had to hand him that. But he lacked the nimble finesse needed to be a truly good cardsharp. "Just don't hold it against me if I don't feel a bit guilty taking your money."

"Not at all," Denton said, shifting his right arm so his hand was pointed in Swill's direction. "Provided you won't hold it against me if I buck you out in gore for giving card slicks a bad name."

"How's that?" Swill asked. He had gone rigid, and the other two locals had the look of ten-year-olds whose hands had been caught in a cookie jar.

"I've run into a lot of cheats in my time," Denton went on. "You're not the worst, but you're damn close to it. You should never try the same trick two hands in a row. That's the mark of an amateur."

Swill slowly pushed his chair back. "Talk like that can get a man killed, gambler."

"So can cheating," Denton said.

One of the other locals chimed in, a brawny specimen in dire need of a bath. "We know Gus Swill real well, mister. He'd never cheat anyone. He's as honest as the year is long."

The gambler grinned. "And you're a bald-faced liar."

Their bluff had been called. Fargo expected them to try for their hardware and they didn't disappoint him. Swill was fastest, but the Smith and Wesson wasn't clear of its holster before Fargo pushed to his feet and filled his hand with his Colt. As he drew he thumbed back the hammer, and at the loud *click* the three locals turned to stone.

Simultaneously, Denton had given his right wrist a flick and a Remington-Eliot .32-caliber four-barrel derringer had slid into his palm. Commonly known as a pepperbox, it had a ring trigger and was quite deadly at short range.

Fargo sidled around the table to come up on Swill from behind. Reaching under the cheat's arm, he relieved Swill of the Smith and Wesson and slid it off across the floor. Then he gripped the wide cuff of Swill's left sleeve, and tugged upward. It rose high enough to reveal a mechanical holdout strapped to Swill's forearm. A similar tug on Swill's other sleeve revealed a second holdout.

"Talk about greedy," Denton said, rising. "What should we do with these jackasses, friend? The last town I was in, they hung a cardsharp from the most convenient tree. And I noticed plenty of trees outside."

Harry Barnes stood and hastily stepped back. "I want you boys to know I had no part in this. I've never swindled a soul in all my born days."

"I'll vouch for that," Mabel said, and treated herself to a more than healthy swallow of rotgut.

Fargo frisked Swill and found a Green River knife, which he tossed into a corner. "Your turn now," he told the cheat's companions, and took a step toward them.

Demonstrating he had more sinew than brains, the brawny tough yelled, "Like hell!" He heaved out of his chair and made a mad grab for a Volcanic Arms brass-plated pistol tucked under his belt.

Fargo lunged, and brought the Colt's barrel crashing down onto the bridge of the man's nose. Cartilage crunched. Blood spurted over the tough's cheeks and jaw as he drew up short, howling in outrage as much as pain.

Fargo relieved him of the pistol, then stepped back. The third man opened his jacket and turned completely around to show he wasn't heeled. Motioning for them to move back, Fargo faced the main culprit.

Gus Swill was as white as high country snow. Beads of sweat had sprouted on his sloping brow, and he nervously licked his pudgy lips. "Don't do anything hasty, mister! Why don't you take the pot and all my winnings and we'll call it even? Divide it up with the gambler, if you like."

"I was planning on doing that anyway," Fargo said. He leveled the Colt at the portly man's ample stomach.

"Don't!" Swill whined, his nerve breaking. "What I did was wrong, sure, but no harm came of it."

Denton came around the table. "Only because we caught you before you walked off with our money, you obscene slug." He jammed the muzzles of the pepperbox against Swill's temple and Swill bleated like a terror-struck goat. "I would be perfectly in my rights to blow a hole in your head."

"Hold on!" Swill cried shrilly. "It ain't right to kill a man over a little thing like cards."

"A little thing?" Denton repeated coldly. "I'll have you know cards are how I make my living. You've not only slandered my profession, you've insulted every honorable gambler alive."

Fargo repressed a grin. Honesty and gambling hardly went hand-in-hand. The simple fact was, most gamblers cheated in some form or another. Some relied on sleight of hand. Others used rings or poker chips with tiny mirrors on them to read cards. Still others preferred marked decks. Then there were those, like Swill, whose fingers weren't nimble enough to deal crookedly without the aid of a holdout.

Swill nervously wiped a sleeve across his forehead. "What is it you want from me? Ask anything and it's yours. My horse. My saddle. My belongings."

"For starters, we'll dispose of your toys," Denton said, and tapped the pepperbox against the holdout on Swill's right forearm.

"Have a heart," Swill said plaintively. "I sent for these from a mail-order outfit. Do you have any notion how much they cost?"

Fargo had seen some of the advertisements in newspapers and on flyers posted in saloons all over the West. The premier supplier of "advantage tools," as they were commonly referred to, was Grandine's of New York City. Grandine's put out an entire catalogue of nothing but marked cards, holdouts, doctored dice, card trimmers, phosphorescent ink, and specially tinted blue glasses to read cards marked with the ink. None of the items were cheap. A single holdout of the kind worn by Swill cost upwards of twenty-five dollars.

"Consider it a lesson learned," Denton said, and wagged the pepperbox. "Shuck them or I'll relieve you of your ears."

"You wouldn't!" Swill blustered.

Denton's left arm flicked and a dagger materialized in his hand. "A riverboat cheat once said the same thing. They call him One-eared Tom now."

Swill sullenly hiked his sleeve higher and began to undo the leather straps that held the holdout in place.

Harry Barnes had retreated to the sanctuary of his bar, while Mabel stood there sipping her drink and grinning at Swill's expense. "What are your brothers going to say when they hear how you crawled?" she taunted.

"Shut up, bitch," Swill snapped, his eyes twin barbs of spite.

"Or what? You'll beat on me like I hear you do that poor filly of yours?" Mabel snorted. "I'd like to see you try. I'll turn you from a steer into a heifer."

"Pardon me, mister. I'm Sam Ziegler. I don't mean to pry, but I'm sort of the closest thing Les Bois has to a civic leader, and it's my duty to try and keep everyone in line." Ziegler poked a thumb northward. "What was that all about?"

"They were cheating at cards," Fargo said.

"Do tell." Ziegler didn't sound the least bit surprised. "I reckon they were bound to get caught sooner or later. The last wagon train that came through, Gus Swill took a pilgrim for pretty near two hundred dollars."

Fargo had little interest in the cheat's accomplishments. He went to go in, but Ziegler wasn't done.

"Has anyone told you about Swill's brothers? He's got eight of 'em and they're all as sidewinder-mean as he is. They live back up in the Seven Devils Mountains. Those fellers he was with, Ike Porter and Tim Gib, are pards of theirs. A dangerous bunch to have mad at you, I can tell you that."

"Thanks for the warning," Fargo said. Denton had already gone in, and he could hear Mabel's high-pitched laughter.

"Some of us don't cotton to the doings around here, is all," Ziegler said. "The Swills and their friends tend to ride roughshod over the rest of us and there's not a whole hell of a lot we can do about it."

"That's too bad." Fargo took another step but stopped at the next words out of the storekeep's mouth.

"You could do something, though. Any hombre who can run off Gus Swill has to have more sand than a desert. What would you say if we offered to hire you to take care of all the Swills?"

Fargo glanced over his shoulder. "Take care of them?"

"Get rid of them permanently," Ziegler elaborated. "Some towns hire regulators to dispose of their vermin. We'd like to do the same." With a wave of his hand, Ziegler included the onlookers. "How would you like the job?"

"This is awful sudden," Fargo commented. They didn't know him from Adam and must be desperate for help.

But just as he wouldn't gun Swill and the others down in cold blood, he had never hired out as an assassin and he wasn't going to start now.

"If you only knew," Ziegler said. "We've been looking for the right man for over a year now. About eight weeks ago we thought we'd found him. A cowboy drifted in from down Texas way. He was a hardcase riding the owl-hoot trail, or so he claimed, and we thought he'd be perfect. We outfitted him with a new rifle and plenty of ammunition and all the grub he'd need, and off into the Devils he went." Ziegler frowned. "He never came back."

"Maybe he was playing you for fools," Fargo said. "Maybe he took that new rifle and kept going."

"We suspected as much," Ziegler said, "until his horse showed up, half-lame and half-starved. The saddle was coated with dry blood." He came closer and lowered his voice. "So what do you say? Between us we can afford to pay you seven hundred dollars. Not a bad grubstake."

Not bad at all, Fargo reflected, and proof they must *really* want the Swills dead. "I'm not your man," he said, and entered the saloon before Ziegler could bend his ear some more. Denton was at the same table, playing solitaire. Mabel and Barnes were at the counter, nursing drinks. Fargo snatched up his glass and walked over for a refill.

"That was mighty nice of you to speak up on my behalf," Mabel thanked him. "I can't recollect the last time a man did that for me."

Fargo leaned on the plank and gave her a new scrutiny. Her breasts were larger than most and swelled against her dress as if trying to burst out. Full hips and nicely shaped thighs were outlined by the silken fabric. His groin twitched at images he conjured of her lying naked in an inviting pose.

Mabel inched up to him and playfully placed a forefinger on his chest. Her eyes hooded, she cooed, "I'd like to thank you for what you did."

"That's not necessary," Fargo assured her.

"Maybe not." Mabel glanced below his belt and rimmed her full lips with the pink tip of her tongue. "But it sure would be a night you'd remember."

2

Mabel's room above the saloon was small but comfortably furnished. She had hung frilly red curtains on the window and thrown a red oval rug on the floor. Her furniture consisted of a rocking chair, a table, and a dresser. Then there was the bed. She had invested in a four-poster that took up half of the floor space. The quilt alone must have cost her half a year's earnings unless she'd made it herself. It was a bright shade of red to match the rest of her color scheme.

"It's not much, but I get by," Mabel said as she closed and bolted the door. Moving past him to the table, she opened a bottle of whiskey and partially filled one of several glasses. "Here. Harry lets me have a bottle a week on the house."

Fargo accepted it and let the coffin varnish burn a warm path down his throat to the pit of his stomach.

"You're the quiet type, aren't you?" Mabel said. "I like that in a man." She raised her glass and clinked it against his. "Here's to you, big man. Thanks again for standing up for me." Mabel gulped the whiskey down, and grinned. "Not bad, eh? And it's not watered down like a lot of the stock Harry sells."

Perfume wreathed her like a cloud. Fargo breathed deep of the honeysuckle fragrance and idly lifted a hand to lightly stroke her scarlet hair.

Mabel's strawberry lips quirked in a lecherous grin. "You had me worried downstairs, handsome. For a minute there I thought you were going to decline my invite."

She pressed against him and said throatily, "I reckon I still have what it takes to make a man forget his cares."

That was only part of the reason Fargo accepted her invitation. The other part had to do with the fact that he needed a place to sleep for the night. Harry Barnes had mentioned there wasn't a spare bed to be had anywhere else. So, after taking the Ovaro to the stable, he had returned to the saloon and agreed to accompany Mabel upstairs.

"I won't have my looks much longer, I'm afraid," Mabel was saying. "A girl in my profession is ready to be put out to pasture at thirty."

"Is that why you stay here?" Fargo asked to hold up his end of the conversation.

Mabel nodded, and poured more red-eye into her glass. "In a big city I would hardly have any customers at all. They'd flock to the younger girls. And I couldn't blame them. I'm past my prime and I'm honest enough to admit it."

"Don't be so hard on yourself. You can still turn a man's head." Fargo sat on the edge of the table. "What will you do when you get to San Francisco?"

"What any dove does when she can't ply her trade. I'll find a nice, decent man somewhere and entice him into marrying me," Mabel said wistfully. "And I'll be a damn good wife, too. He'll never regret tying the knot."

"I'll bet he won't," Fargo said.

"What a sweet thing to say." Mabel leaned against him and traced the outline of his left ear with a long fingernail. "You're a romantic at heart. I can tell. I bet you haven't had much experience with women like me."

Fargo chose not to disillusion her. "I've had a little," he hedged. More than he could count in a month of Sundays.

"You're a nice change of pace. I'm sick and tired of the men around here. They don't believe in small talk. A few grunts, a few shoves, and it's over. They bore me silly."

"I'll try to keep you interested," Fargo said dryly.

Mabel tweaked his earlobe. "I was hoping you or that

gambler would be inclined to a romp in the hay. He's a gentleman, too. Tipped his hat to me, he did, when he came into the saloon. You could have floored me with a feather. I can't remember the last time a man did that." She pecked his cheek lightly. "He's bound for San Francisco, too. Something about a big card game he wants to take part in."

Setting down his glass, Fargo placed his hands on her hips.

"Lute Denton is his full name," Mabel babbled on. "He says he's from down New Orleans way. I reckon he'll bed down at the stable for the night. Poor man, having to sleep in all that smelly hay."

Fargo was beginning to get the idea she was smitten. It didn't surprise him. Gamblers had a certain allure that attracted females like a flame attracts moths. Maybe it was the air of risk and danger they had about them. His gambler friends never had any trouble finding a willing companion when they wanted one. As one of them, Kansas Jack, liked to joke, "It's the frock coats and black hats. Hooks the ladies every time."

"But enough about him," Mabel said, and polished off her second glass. She had a capacity for alcohol most men would envy. "Let's talk about you some. Tell me something about yourself."

"Anything?"

"Anything at all," Mabel nodded. "Your past. The present. Your likes and your dislikes."

"I don't much like talking about myself," Fargo informed her.

Cackling, Mabel smacked him on the shoulder. "Don't beat around the bush, do you? Fair enough. I'll shut up if that's what you want."

"What I want," Fargo said, suddenly bending and scooping her into his arms, "is you flat on your back." He carried her to the four-poster and dropped her on the quilt.

Mabel squealed in delight, then rolled onto her side, propped her head up in her hand, and crooked a delicate eyebrow. "Want me to undress myself or will you do the honors? The yokels around here usually let me do it because they can't figure out how to get my clothes off without help—" She suddenly hushed up as hooves drummed loudly out in front.

Fargo moved to the window and parted the curtains. Two men he had never seen were dismounting at the hitch rail below. Both were in their twenties and nicely dressed in tailored suits and hats. Their mounts were fine bays, their saddles costly rigs few ordinary souls could afford. Judging by their similar features, they were related. Brothers, possibly. Before entering, they took the time to swat the trail dust from their clothes, and while doing so, one exposed a revolver in a shoulder holster. The other brother, Fargo saw, had a bulge under his arm as well. They scanned the other buildings, then went into the tavern.

"Must be some of the local boys," Mabel said without getting up to see. "We get five or six a night here, except on Saturdays when the place is packed."

"I didn't know there were that many settlers in the area," Fargo commented. He was about to let go of the curtains when the so-called mayor, Sam Ziegler, came running out of the general store and over to the hitch rail. Ziegler examined the bays, glanced all around, and reached up to unfasten a saddlebag.

If there was one thing Fargo despised more than a card cheat, it was a thief. He was going to rap on the window to warn Ziegler off, when the grizzled oldster looked sharply off to the north, took a quick step back, then whirled and raced for the general store as if the demons of hell were nipping at his heels. Seconds later, more hooves hammered and four newcomers appeared. Their grungy clothes identified them as locals. Neither Gus Swill, Porter, nor Gib were among them. Fargo turned to the bed.

Mabel had folded back the pink quilt and now lay back on the smooth white sheet. She had slid both ribbon-thin straps off her shoulders, and was undoing the stays to her dress. It had slid partway down her oversized breasts, and her twin melons were on the verge of popping free.

Fargo grinned. "And you claim I'm the one who doesn't like to beat around the bush?"

Giggling, Mabel crooked a finger. "Come on over here and I'll show you a whole different kind of bush. Turn down the lamp while you're at it. I like to make love in the dark."

Fargo obliged her even though he preferred the light. He left enough of a glow to cast the room in pale relief. Unstrapping his gunbelt, he placed it on the floor within easy reach, then sat with one knee bent, facing her.

"You sure are a fine-looking son-of-a-gun," Mabel said. "How is it a lovely young gal hasn't roped you yet?"

"I run too fast."

It was a full minute before Mabel stopped laughing and placed a warm hand on his. "You sure know how to make a woman feel good inside. That's a rare trait nowadays."

"I'm just getting started." Fargo molded his mouth to hers. Her lips were deliciously soft and tasted like sugar. He delved his tongue between her upper and lower teeth and was greeted by her own in a satiny swirl of tingling sensation.

Some women kissed like lumps of coal, but not Mabel. She put her heart into it. She ran her tongue along his gums, she bit gently on his lips, she sucked on his tongue. All the while her fingers were exploring. Hitching at his shirt, she slipped her left hand up underneath it and rubbed his corded midriff in tantalizing circles.

Fargo's manhood stirred and hardened. Soon he had a bulge that his buckskin pants could scarcely contain. His breath caught in his throat when Mabel's right hand cupped him, low down. She knew just what to do in order to incite him to a fevered pitch and she wasn't shy about doing it. A knot formed in his throat, and his member began to pulse with pent-up need.

"*Mmmmmm,*" Mabel cooed. "Evidently not all the redwoods are in California."

Fargo wasn't idle either. He eased her dress to her waist and covered each of her wonderful breasts with a

17

hungry hand. She squirmed when he tweaked her upright nipples. She gasped when he pinched one, hard, and pulled on it. And she panted in his ear when he abruptly shoved a knee between her thighs and brushed his knee-cap against her nether region.

"You're getting me hot, lover."

That was the general idea, Fargo mused, as he nibbled on her lower lip while continuing to massage her twin globes. She scooted her bottom against him and ground her hips in an age-old invitation.

Fargo felt her fingers pry at his pants. Then they were inside and she was holding him, flesh to flesh, skin to skin. She stroked him lightly, her touch as delicate as a flower. The constriction in Fargo's throat grew and he had to consciously keep himself from prematurely exploding.

"I can't wait to get your pole inside of me," Mabel said in a husky voice.

Fargo couldn't wait, either. He started to peel off her dress. She helped him slide it down over her hips, then wriggled it to her knees and kicked it off with a flip of her right leg. Her undergarments, the few she wore, were shed next, and presently Fargo feasted on the vision of her bare body. Huge breasts arched out over a stomach that was still flat and firm, and her thighs were as smooth as glass. He sculpted her left melon with one hand while his other caressed her nether regions.

Mabel's fiery breath fanned his ear. "I'm so ready for you," she whispered.

Fargo ran a hand up one thigh and down another. In reflex, her legs parted and she curled them around his hips. He kissed her cheek, her forehead, then glued his lips to hers. Mabel's nipples poked like nails against his chest, and when he squeezed her right breast, she arched her spine and nearly lifted him off the bed.

Ever-so-slowly, Fargo rubbed his forefinger across her moist slit. At the contact of his finger with her tiny knob, Mabel cried out softly. Her fingernails raked his shoulders and upper back.

"Do that again, lover!"

Fargo was all too happy to oblige. He flicked his finger back and forth until she was trembling in ecstasy. Suddenly he shoved his finger up into her womanhood, all the way to the knuckle. Mabel went as taut as wire. She clung to him, devouring his mouth with hers while thrusting her backside against his hand again and again and again. Fargo matched her tempo, stroking her with two fingers. Every plunge elicited a low moan. He kept at it, drawing out the pleasure, hers and his.

Without warning, Mabel let go and started to swing her body around. Fargo understood why when her knees nestled his head between them and her hair brushed his thighs. The next moment an exquisite thrill coursed through his body. Her mouth was where her hand had been.

Now it was Fargo who arched his back and gasped. His self-control slipped and he had to gird himself against his body's natural tendency. Mabel dallied for an eternity, licking him from bottom to top and back again. He was surprised and not a little disappointed when she abruptly stopped and pushed him onto his back. Her motive became clear as she rose up onto her knees, swivelled to face him, and straddled his chest.

A mischievous grin lit Mabel's face. "I've liked to ride since I was sixteen," she joked, and with a smooth motion, she impaled herself on him as neatly as could be.

. They both stiffened. Fargo could feel her wet inner walls contract around his manhood like a velvet glove. He drove upward, ramming himself up into her core, and Mabel vented a long, low groan.

"*Ohhhhhhhh.* I could do this forever."

So could Fargo. Pacing himself, he continued driving into her for long minutes on end. She countered every stroke with one of her own. They were fused at the hips, their two bodies one. Together, they rose toward the carnal summit of their mutual cravings.

Fargo might have held out longer if not for a trick Mabel resorted to. She contracted her magnificently soft tunnel even more. He tried not to explode, but his body wouldn't be denied. He shook from head to toe, and the room blurred into a golden haze. At the same instant, Fargo cried out and gushed.

The bed shook under them. The four hardwood legs slapped the floor in a steady cadence. Fargo didn't know if the racket could be heard downstairs, and he didn't much care. The moment was all that counted, the moment, and the profound sense of unbelievable rapture that swept over him.

How long he coasted on the precipice of consciousness, Fargo couldn't rightly say. He was vaguely aware of Mabel still pumping on top of him, of her heavy breasts on his chest, of tiny breaths fluttering across his neck. He draped an arm across her back and closed his eyes.

"I hope you're up for a second helping in a spell," Mabel panted. "I never have been satisfied with a single portion."

Just then loud shouts broke out below. An argument was taking place in the saloon. Someone swore a mean streak and a revolver boomed, not once but four times. All four slugs punched up through Mabel's floor, missing her bed by inches, and thudded into her ceiling.

"My God!" Mabel exclaimed. "They'll hit us if they're not careful."

The arguing continued, louder than before, but not quite loud enough for Fargo to make out what was being said. Sitting up, he slid off the bed and hurriedly commenced dressing.

"Where are you off to?"

Without warning a fifth slug ripped through the floor and struck the dresser, digging a furrow across two of the oak drawers. "Need you ask?" Fargo rejoined. Swiftly, he buckled on his Colt and was out the door and down a short flight of stairs in a rush. They opened onto a corner of the saloon. He stopped in the shadows, able to see without being seen, and took stock of the situation.

Lute Denton was at a table playing cards alone, and had stopped to watch the proceedings.

Harry Barnes was behind the counter. He looked as if someone had just kicked him in his oysters.

At the far end of the bar stood the two well-dressed young men. Both were plainly angry, and their hands were poised to dip under their jackets.

Facing them were the four locals who had arrived a while ago. Three had their backs to Fargo. The fourth lounged against the plank while casually reloading a Prescott single-action Navy revolver. Gunsmoke curled in the air above him, only a few inches below the holes he had shot in the ceiling.

"Please, Clancy," Harry Barnes was saying. "You can't go shooting up my place. Someone might get hurt."

The man named Clancy was a lean hardcase with a hooked nose and dark, beady eyes. He wore a brown shirt, clean jeans, and polished boots, and had adorned his hat with a leather band. He obviously thought highly of himself. "I wasn't aiming to hurt anyone," he responded, and gave the Prescott a twirl into its holster. "I was just showing these Eastern boys how we kill flies in our neck of the woods."

Barnes stared upward, and blanched. "You don't understand. Mabel's room is right above this one."

"So?" Clancy responded. "What's one whore, more or less? It's not as if she can do anything about it."

The four locals chuckled.

Fargo picked that moment to make his entrance. "Maybe she can't do anything, but I sure as hell can."

Clancy's three partners whirled. One was a beefy character in an elk-hide vest and raccoon cap. Another was short but as wide as a wagon. The third was a buck-toothed kid not much past sixteen. They were armed with various revolvers, except the short one who had a Sharps rifle slung across his broad back.

Clancy wasn't the least bit alarmed. Looking up, he said in amusement, "Well, well. What have we here? What's your stake in this, busybody?"

Harry Barnes cleared his throat and came along the bar toward Fargo, saying, "I'd like you to meet four more of the Swill boys. Clancy, there, is lightning with a pistol. Shem can hit a plug of tobacco at two hundred yards with that Sharps of his. The guy in the raccoon hat, Wilt, is the best trapper this side of the Mississippi. And Billy is the youngest of the bunch."

Fargo took another step to the right to have clear shots at all four. "And between them they don't have the brains of a pile of horseshit."

Clancy's eyes narrowed and he slowly unfurled. His brothers moved to either side as he strode past them, his arms loose at his sides. "We don't take kindly to insults. If you don't—" Catching himself, he glanced at Harry Barnes. "What did you mean just now by this jasper meeting 'more' of us Swills? Who else has he met?"

"One of your other brothers," Fargo said when it was apparent Barnes was too scared to answer. "Gus, his name was. He tried to cheat me at cards and I had to pound some sense into him. I'm surprised you didn't run into him on the way here."

"We didn't come by the usual trail," Clancy said, and smirked. "Mister, you must be loco to come right out and tell us like you did. Or ain't you heard? Hurt one Swill and you have the rest of us down on your head. We're not about to let you get away with what you did."

"It's not your brother you should be concerned about."

"How so?" Clancy mocked him.

"The question for you to answer," Fargo said, with a bob of his chin at the entrance, "is how you're going to make it out that door in one piece."

Clancy had it, then. Slowly nodding, he said, "I'll be damned. The last jackass who prodded me is buried off under the trees in an unmarked grave." His sallow countenance lit with sadistic delight. "Mind telling me why you have such a powerful hankering to die?"

"Ask the flies," Fargo said.

Clancy's gaze drifted to the ceiling. "You were upstairs with the cow? Is that what this is about? Did I intrude on your diddling?"

Billy Swill brayed with mirth. Shem had his big hands on the strap to his Sharps, while Wilt had laid hold of the bone hilt of a long-bladed skinning knife.

"Can't you count, mister?" Clancy said. "It's four to one. You can't hope to drop all of us before we drop you. Be smart. Crawl out of here on your hands and knees and maybe we'll let you live."

"You've got it backward."

"Enough of this jackass," Billy fumed, and lowered his hand toward his Merwin and Hulbert Army revolver. He froze at a stern order from his older brother.

Clancy's puzzlement was as transparent as glass. "Just you against the four of us?" he stressed. Clancy was no fool. He appeared to be the brains of the Swill clan and wasn't about to light the fuse until he was sure things would go their way.

"Let's shoot this yack and be done with him," Billy urged. "I came here to drink, not listen to this randy spout nonsense."

The saloon grew quiet. Everyone was waiting for Clancy Swill to make a decision. In the sudden silence, the smack of one of Lute Denton's cards on the table was unnaturally loud. "Speaking for myself, gentlemen," he said good-naturedly, "I hope you simpletons do make a play for your hardware. It will give me quite a tale to tell when I get to San Francisco." He smacked down another card. "Why, the newspapers there might be interested enough to print an account. I can see the headlines now." He held his hand up and moved it from right to left as if reading the banner. *Trailsman Guns Down Pack Of Idiots.*

"Trailsman?" Clancy Swill said. Uncertainty tinged with disbelief replaced his confusion. "That feller we've heard so much about? The one who killed Blue Raven, the renegade? And had that run-in with Dunn, the paid assassin? The same Trailsman who took part in that sharpshooting match down to Springfield, Missouri?"

The gambler nodded. "One and the same, yes. I was in the audience that day. I saw Vin Chadwell, Buck Smith, and Dottie Wheatridge vie with Fargo, there, for the top prize. Four of the best sharpshooters in the whole country." He whistled softly at the memory. "I never met anyone before or since who can match them. Fargo shot five clothespins off a line at twenty-five yards, and did it so fast, I only missed it because I blinked."

Billy Swill wasn't buying the account. "Like hell! You're trying to spook us. No one is as good as you make this galoot out to be."

"Try him and find out," Lute Denton suggested, and grinned.

"Billy!" Clancy cautioned.

The youth bent forward, his right hand hooked near the butt of his Army revolver. "Stay out of this, big brother. I aim to call this Trailsman's bluff, and there ain't a damn thing you can do about it."

Fargo's fight wasn't with the bucktoothed youngster. Clancy was the one whose carelessness had nearly cost Mabel and him their lives. "Go home to your mother, boy," he said, and instantly realized it had been the wrong thing to say.

A feral snarl erupted from Billy Swill's throat and he stabbed for his six-gun. He wasn't slow, but he wasn't anywhere near fast enough, either.

Fargo had his Colt out and level almost before Billy Swill's fingers wrapped around the Merwin and Hulbert revolver. He fired once, from the hip.

The slug bored Billy Swill high in the right shoulder and spun him completely around. The Army revolver went flying.

For a moment shock riveted the rest of the Swills in place. Then Billy took a faltering step toward Clancy, and pitched toward the floor. Clancy and Shem caught him, but Clancy promptly let go and spun toward Fargo, fury turning him reckless. "You shot my brother, you son of a bitch!"

"I can do the same for the rest of you," Fargo said, and slid his Colt back into his holster, implicitly inviting them to try him.

Clancy's right arm twitched, and for a few tense moments it seemed he would go for his own hogleg. Then, with an obvious effort, he unwound and barked, "Shem! Wilt! Bring Billy. He'll need doctoring."

"But—" Shem began.

"Just do it!" Clancy stormed toward the door and held it open for his brothers. As they sullenly filed past, he gave Fargo a look that would wither a cactus. "I don't care how famous you are. You just made the biggest mistake of your life. No one puts lead into a Swill and lives to brag about it." He slowly backed out. "The newspapers will have a story to print, sure enough. But the headline will read, 'Trailsman Dies In Seven Devils Country.'"

3

Skye Fargo almost always woke up at first light. It was a habit formed as the result of years spent on the trail, where it was important that he be in the saddle by sunup in order to cover more distance before night. So it was, that as a pale tinge faintly lit Mabel's curtains, Fargo quietly rolled out of bed, dressed, and gathered up his belongings. His saddlebags over his left shoulder, his Henry rifle in his right hand, he glanced one last time at Mabel, who slumbered peacefully on. She had been right. It had been a night he would long remember. The man she eventually snared would have no need to complain.

Easing the door open, Fargo slipped out and closed it behind him. The stairs creaked, but that couldn't be helped. The saloon was empty, and chill. Harry Barnes had a small room off behind the bar, and from it came thunderous snoring.

Grinning, Fargo walked around the counter, opened a bottle of whiskey, and took a long, healthy drink. It would suffice in lieu of coffee. He replaced the bottle and crossed to the door, his spurs jingling softly. Opening it, he took a step—and stopped dead.

The two young men who had arrived the previous evening were leaning against the hitch rail. They were dressed in the same fancy suits. One had his arms folded, his right hand under his jacket, while the other, who was slightly younger, was gazing off toward the mountains. Both straightened and turned.

"We've been waiting for you, Mr. Fargo," the older one said.

"Mr. Barnes told us you planned on leaving early this morning," the younger one revealed.

Fargo shut the door. "What's so important that you got up before sunrise to talk to me?"

"I'm Jack Carter," the older one said. He was about twenty-five and had frank brown eyes and neatly trimmed brown hair. "This is my brother, John. We're from Ohio."

"You're a long way from home," Fargo commented.

"Don't we know it." Like his younger sibling, Jack Carter appeared tired and trail-worn. They had the look of men who had been on the go for a very long time and it was catching up to them. "But not by choice. You see, we're searching for our sister, Suzanne. She was with a wagon train bound for Oregon. Her, and her new husband."

John took up the account when Jack paused. "Suzanne disappeared from the train three months ago, southwest of here along the Snake River."

"Disappeared?" Fargo asked quizzically. Women on wagon trains were usually well-guarded and knew better than to stray too far afield.

"Sis had gone with some other ladies to wash clothes in the river," Jack related. "A man went with them to keep watch. But somehow Susie up and vanished right out from under their noses."

"Strange," Fargo said. The earth doesn't just open up and swallow people.

"It's more than that," John said. "It had to be deliberate on someone's part. Susie would never go off by herself. We've talked to some of the women who were there, and they say that one minute she was by the bank, washing her husband's shirts. The next she was gone."

"The women called her name over and over," Jack said, "and when she didn't answer, a general cry was raised. Nearly everyone on the wagon train helped search the area. The wagon boss even held the train over an extra day. But they never found any trace of her."

"No one found tracks?" Fargo's first thought was that a grizzly or mountain lion had jumped her and dragged the body off. A single blow from a bear's paw or one bite from a cougar's powerful jaws were enough to kill. Often, they struck so quickly that the victim had no time to cry out.

"That's the strangest part of all," Jack said. "They couldn't find so much as a single footprint. They had a frontiersman with them, a man by the name of Tanager—"

"I know him," Fargo interrupted. Dan Tanager worked as a guide and army scout on occasion. A former trapper, Tanager had lived with the Crows for a score of years, and was as competent as frontiersmen came.

"Tanager couldn't find any tracks either," Jack disclosed. "We talked to him out in Portland. He's a feisty old cuss, and he told us he'd never seen anything like it. He spent six or seven hours going over every square inch of ground for acres around and there wasn't a trace of Susie anywhere. It was as if she had blinked out of existence."

"I'm sorry for your loss," Fargo said. He had an idea where this was leading, but he inquired anyway. "What does all of this have to do with me?"

Jack Carter came closer. "We were up late talking to Mr. Denton, the gambler. He says you're one of the best scouts in the country. That you spent time among the Sioux. That you can track anyone, anywhere, anytime."

"It's been three months," Fargo reminded them. "Whatever sign there was has long since been wiped out." He started toward the stable. "I know what you want, but you're asking the impossible."

John Carter stepped in front of him, barring his way. "Please, Mr. Fargo. You're our last hope. We've spent months hunting down all the people we could who were there that day. We've been to the spot ourselves half a dozen times. All we want is for you to take a look. It's not all that far."

"Thirty miles, at least," Fargo mentioned. A two day

ride, even if they pushed their horses, over some very rough terrain.

"We know we'd be imposing," Jack said, "but we can't give up hope, not so long as there's a slim chance our sister is still alive." He paused, and when he spoke next, he was choked with emotion. "The three of us were real close as kids. We love Susie, Mr. Fargo. What kind of brothers would we be if we didn't do all we could to find out what happened to her?"

"Haven't you ever cared for anyone?" John pressed their appeal. "Would you give up if it were your sister?"

Fargo felt sorry for them. He truly did. But they were grasping at straws. If there had been tracks or sign of any kind, Dan Tanager would have found it. "I'd like to help. But I'd only be wasting my time and yours."

"How about if we make it worth your while?" Jack said. Reaching into an inside jacket pocket, he pulled out a wallet. As he did, Fargo again glimpsed the butt of a revolver in a shoulder holster. "Would two hundred dollars change your mind?" Opening the wallet, he produced a sheath of bills half an inch thick and peeled off the stated amount.

Fargo hesitated, thinking of Mabel. Two hundred dollars would get her to San Francisco and give her enough to live on until she could find a job.

"Three hundred then?" Jack Carter said, peeling off more. "All you have to do to earn it is spend a few hours looking over the site where Suzanne vanished."

"Did you two rob a bank somewhere?" Fargo stalled. He was strongly tempted, but he had an appointment to keep with a man in the Willamette Valley.

"We're rather well-to-do," Jack answered. "Our father owns a string of businesses throughout Ohio. He couldn't come with us because he's in poor health." Jack peeled off more bills. "Four hundred is my top offer."

Leaning the Henry against his leg, Fargo accepted the money. "Two days there. One day to look around. That's the best I can do."

"A whole day?" Jack said, brightening. "That's more

than we dared hope. But people tell us if anyone can find anything, it's you."

Fargo folded the bills and shoved them into a pocket. A certain house of ill repute in Portland would merit a visit on his way to the Willamette Valley. "Why didn't you ask Dan Tanager to help?"

"We did, but he refused," John said. "He told us we were wasting our time. That if he couldn't find her right after she vanished, he sure as hell couldn't find her now."

Jack gestured at the pair of bays. "We can head out as soon as you're ready. Don't worry about provisions. Our pack animals are hidden up the trail a piece, where we camped for the night."

"Why didn't you bring them into Les Bois?" Fargo wondered aloud.

The brothers exchanged glances. "Let's just say we deemed it best, and let it go at that," the oldest replied.

"Give me a minute. I'll be right back." Fargo reentered the saloon. Loud snoring still issued from the back room. He took the stairs three at a stride and opened Mabel's door without knocking. She was curled up on her side, her red hair splashed across her cheek. In repose her face was smooth and innocent. He counted out two hundred dollars and laid the bills out near her pillow.

The Carter boys were mounted and waiting over by the stable when Fargo re-emerged. He claimed his saddle and bridle from the tack room where he had left them the night before, and within minutes had the stallion saddled. A golden glow bathed the eastern horizon as he lightly tapped his spurs to the pinto's sides and trotted south from the settlement.

The Carters were grinning like kids whose fondest birthday wish had been granted. Half a mile down the trail they reined to the right and proceeded on through white pines to a clearing where two pack horses had been picketed. In the center was the charred remains of a campfire. Four large bulging packs had been left propped against the bole of a tree.

"You took a gamble leaving everything here," Fargo commented. A bear would make short shrift of the packs.

And a roving warrior would be more than happy to help themselves to the horses.

"We didn't know if we'd run into the Swills," Jack said as he and his brother set to work loading their supplies. "We wanted our hands free, just in case."

"They tried to prod us into a fight," John referred to the saloon incident. "Clancy Swill fired those shots into the ceiling to show off. To demonstrate what he would do to us if we weren't careful."

Fargo had gone back up to Mabel's room after the Swill clan departed and never heard the full story. "What was that all about, anyway?"

"Your guess is as good as ours," Jack said, engrossed in tying down a pack. "We came up this way to ask around and see if anyone had heard anything about Susie. We're convinced she's still alive. Call it crazy, but we both have a feeling we just can't shake."

John nodded vigorously. "We've had it since we first heard the news. Susie *is* alive. I just know she is. She was taken by hostiles and is being held in a village somewhere."

Fargo admired their devotion but he couldn't help but think they were deluding themselves. The Kalispels and Flatheads to the east and the Yakimas and Spokanes to the west were at peace with the whites. Numerous smaller tribes called the region home, but none, so far as he was aware, were on the warpath, or had ever taken a white woman captive. They might indulge in a little horse stealing, but that was about it.

"We had heard about Les Bois from Tanager, the old scout," Jack mentioned. "When we got there, Harry Barnes was nice enough, but he wasn't any help. Then the Swill brothers came in. Barnes told them who we were and why we were there. That's when the trouble began."

"Billy Swill started insulting us," John said. "He claimed we were stupid to believe our sister was still breathing after all this time. He made fun of our clothes, calling us a pair of 'citified dudes.' His exact words."

Fargo frowned. In some quarters hazing greenhorns

was a popular sport, but it was not one with which he agreed.

"I told that buck-toothed hooligan that at least we know how to bathe regularly," John related, "and he became quite upset. He was going to take a swing at me, but Clancy stepped in. He swore at us, and when we wouldn't go for our guns, he accused us of being yellow."

"I assured them we didn't want any trouble, but it didn't do any good," Jack Carter said. "They didn't seem to care. All that mattered to them was putting us in our place. Along about then was when Clancy whipped out his revolver and shot at the flies on the ceiling. He hit three of them, too. Best shooting I ever did see."

"Then you came down," John concluded, "and put them in their place. They're liable to skin you alive if they ever get their hands on you."

"They can try," Fargo said. He wouldn't lose sleep worrying. In the wild he was in his element, and if the Swills came after him, they would regret it.

Soon the brothers were ready. Each of them grabbed hold of the lead rope to one of the pack animals and filed toward the trail. Jack assumed the lead.

The sun was half an hour high, the forest alive with the chirping and warbling of a legion of birds. A jay squawked at Fargo from high in a fir. An orange-and-black butterfly flitted by on gossamer wings. Further on, a rabbit bolted out almost from under the Ovaro's hooves.

Fargo smiled. To others the forest was a frightening realm of savage beasts and doubly savage men, but to him they were home. Most of his adult life had been spent roaming where few others had ever roamed before. He had spent more nights under the stars than under a roof. And he wouldn't have it any other way.

As they rode, the Carter brothers revealed more about themselves. They were from Cincinnati. They had been raised on a thirty acre estate, and had gone off to Syracuse University after completing high school. Jack had followed in his father's footsteps and now helped oversee the family's lucrative business enterprises. John had become a lawyer, much to his father's disappointment, and was making a name for himself.

A year ago, Suzanne, the youngest, had married the son of another prominent local businessman, Tom Maxwell. Perhaps to show he was as capable as her father, Maxwell took it into his head to travel to the Promised Land, as Oregon was widely known, and build a business empire of his own. "The land of opportunity," he proclaimed to everyone who would listen, and succeeded in sweet-talking Suzanne into going along.

"We tried to convince her not to go," Jack said over a shoulder, "but she had taken Maxwell for better or for worse, and she was bound to do her wifely duty come hell or high water."

John swore under his breath. "But even Maxwell couldn't be bothered to help us! Like Tanager, he felt it was a waste of time. It's only been three measly months, and Maxwell has already forgotten about her."

"But we haven't," Jack declared. "And we never will, not so long as there's a thread of hope."

By the middle of the afternoon they were winding down out of the range region onto the arid Columbia Plateau. They came to the crest of a barren hill and Fargo took the occasion to draw rein. "Hold up," he said, and shifted in his saddle. He had been watching their back trail all day, and now his instincts were rewarded with a pinpoint of light approximately a mile away. "We're being followed."

Jack had climbed down and was bending to examine his bay's left front hoof. "Are you sure?" he asked, anxiously scouring the landscape. "I don't see anyone. Who do you think it is?"

"Maybe it's that gambler," John said. "He was going to leave Les Bois today or tomorrow."

"It could be anyone," was Jack's assessment. "Harry Barnes told us there are thirty or more homesteads back off in the woods. Cabins, mostly, although he swore that one family lives in a cave."

Fargo turned around. At the base of the hill the trail meandered past a dry wash high enough for his purpose.

"I want the two of you to go on ahead. I'll join you later. If I haven't caught up by nightfall, pitch camp, but keep the fire low. Don't sit next to it, and don't turn your back to the dark."

"You sound like you expect someone to jump us," Jack Carter said.

"Better safe than sorry," Fargo responded. The precautions he had suggested were simple ones every frontiersman worthy of the name heeded. Precautions most any Indian would take. But the majority of whites were far too careless for their own good. They kindled fires large enough to be seen for miles off. They sat close to their fires for warmth, making excellent targets. And, worst of all, they stared into the flames, not off and away from them. If attacked, they would be blinded for the crucial five or ten seconds it took their eyes to adjust to the darkness around them.

"Why can't we stay with you?" John asked. "We have a vested interest in keeping you alive."

"I want whoever is following us to see your tracks," Fargo explained. He rode with them to the base of the hill, then another fifty yards or so along the edge of the wash, at which point he reined sharply down to the bottom and on around a bend.

John waved and hollered, "Be careful!"

Fargo listened to the dull clomp of their receding hoofbeats. Sliding from the saddle, he shucked the Henry from its scabbard. Small stones and loose dirt speckled the sides of the wash, and he was careful not to slip as he climbed to the rim. He hunkered just below it. The spot he had chosen couldn't be seen from the top of the hill, but he could see the crest clearly enough.

Fargo made himself as comfortable as he could and settled down to wait. He thought about Suzanne Maxwell, about how devastated her brothers would be if he couldn't help them find the explanation to her disappearance. But it wasn't unheard of for people to vanish. A husband went off to chop firewood and was never seen again. An Indian maiden left her village to pick berries, and all that was ever found was her basket. Children bounded into the forest to play and never returned.

Nature was a cruel mistress. The price of survival was eternal vigilance. A single blunder, however minor, was enough to turn a healthy, living person into maggot bait. The hunter who tried to cross a frozen lake when the ice wasn't thick enough; the climber who missed a handhold midway up a cliff; the warrior whose bowstring snapped as he was bearing down on an angry bull buffalo. They were vivid examples of strokes of bad luck that ended in death.

Fargo had survived for as long as he had because he never took risks unless he had no other choice. He always did whatever best increased his odds of greeting the next dawn. Granted, there were exceptions, as there were to any rules of thumb, but if there was one thing living in the wild had taught him, it was to look before he leaped—as the old saw had it.

The sun gradually arced higher. Twenty minutes to half an hour had gone by when Fargo heard hoofbeats again. Only these were approaching from the north, at a gallop. Two horses, he reckoned. Ducking low, Fargo removed his hat. There was no need to keep his eyes on the hill. Its shadow splayed across the wash, and it wasn't long before the shadows of the two riders seemed to rise up out of it, and then halted.

Fargo imagined they were surveying the country ahead. He wasn't worried about being spotted. The walls of the wash were too steep, and the bend concealed the Ovaro. Hoofbeats resumed, moving slower this time. Fargo heard voices growing louder by the second.

"—done it back in the mountains," someone was griping. "It's too open now. He'll be harder to pick off."

"Not at night, he won't," said the second man. "We'll wait until they've gathered around their fire. My Sharps will drop him where he sits."

Shem Swill, Fargo deduced, curling his finger around the Henry's trigger. The other had to be one of Shem's brothers.

"I just don't like it, is all," said the griper. "Why didn't Clancy take care of this hombre his own self? Why did he send us?"

"Because you're the best tracker in the family, Wilt," Shem responded, "and I'm the best rifle shot."

Wilt muttered a few words Fargo didn't quite catch, then declared, "I still say we're taking a chance. This Fargo fella is famous. If we kill him, some of his friends might come nosing around. And the last thing we want is to draw attention to ourselves."

"Famous or not, the bastard shot Billy," Shem said. "No one hurts a Swill without paying dearly. An eye for an eye, a tooth for a tooth, remember?"

They were close enough now for Fargo to hear one of them spit. He tensed his legs, intending to wait until they were right on top of him, and then spring out. Movement out of the corner of his eye called for a change in plan. The Ovaro had strayed a few feet past the bend toward him. In another few seconds the Swills would spot it, and be forewarned. Jamming the Henry's stock against his right shoulder, he leapt up over the rim. "Looking for someone, gents?"

Shem and Wilt Swill were twenty-five feet away. Shem had the big Sharps slung across his back. Wilt was armed with his bone-handled skinning knife and an old Colt Walker revolver. They reined up, Shem automatically starting to unsling his rifle. But he thought better of the idea when Fargo thumbed the Henry's hammer back.

"You again!" Wilt exclaimed.

"What's the meaning of this?" Shem blustered. "Do you always go around pointing guns at folks for no reason?"

Swinging the Henry from one to the other and back again, Fargo slowly advanced. "I call planning to bush-whack a man reason enough." He should shoot them where they sat. He had the right. West of the Mississippi, every man was his own judge, jury, and executioner. "Go for your guns. I'll give you more of a chance than you were fixing to give me."

Shem reached for the Sharps.

"Don't!" Wilt said. "He's bluffing. If we keep our hands off our hardware, he won't do a damn thing."

"Are you sure?" Shem asked uncertainly.

"Clancy has been asking around about this feller," Wilt said. "And everyone tells him the same thing. This Fargo character ain't no killer. Not unless he's provoked." Wilt smugly smiled and raised his hands into the air. "Go ahead, mister," he challenged. "Put a hole into me. I dare you."

Fargo shot him.

The slug cored Wilt Swill's shoulder in almost the exact same spot Billy Swill had been hit. The impact catapulted Wilt from his saddle and he tumbled to the ground in a whirl of limbs. His raccoon hat went flying. So did his revolver. He landed with an audible *thud* on his head and shoulders, and didn't move. His horse shied, prancing off to the west a few dozen yards.

"You killed him, you stinking son of a bitch!" Shem railed. But mad as he was, he wasn't rash enough to attempt to unlimber his rifle.

Working the Henry's lever, Fargo fed a new cartridge into the chamber. He had a near-overpowering urge to stroke the trigger again, but instead he marched up to Shem's dun and without saying a word, slammed the Henry against Shem's knee.

"Damn you!" Shem howled in torment and bent down to clutch his leg.

Instantly, Fargo smashed the Henry's stock against the backwoodsman's jaw. Teeth crunched, blood spurted, and Shem pitched face-first into the dirt.

Fargo grabbed the dun's reins, turned the animal completely around, and gave it a sharp smack on the rump. It did what most any horse would do; uttering a loud whinny, it bolted for home. Wilt's sorrel was close behind. Over the hill they raced, their manes and tails flying.

Wheeling, Fargo bent over Shem and relieved him of the Sharps. He flung it far down the wash, then gave

Wilt's big revolver and the bone-handled skinning knife the same treatment. Next he retrieved the Ovaro and sat on a flat rock to wait for the brothers to revive.

Shem came to first. Groaning and spitting blood, he slowly sat up and growled. "If it's the last thing I ever do, I'll hunt you down and kill you."

"The Swills never learn, do they?" Fargo said. His rifle was propped on the rock beside him. He drew the Colt, instead, and calmly planted a slug in Shem Swill's left thigh.

For most, that would have been enough to send them into agonized convulsions. But not Shem. From under his vest he flourished a knife of his own, and with a roar of rage he heaved onto one knee and lunged.

4

Skye Fargo wasn't a cold-blooded murderer. He never killed unless he had to. But some people would say the Swills had given him more than just cause. He had heard them plotting to bushwhack him. But the way Fargo saw it, if he simply gunned them down, he was no different than they were. So he did the next best thing. He shot them, but he didn't aim to kill, only to wound. He was trying to get it through their thick heads that if they tried to kill him, they would regret it. But some folks just never learned.

Shem Swill's leg was spurting scarlet, but the enraged hardcase didn't care. Lips drawn back from his shattered front teeth, he swung his knife in a vicious arc. "Die, you bastard! Die!"

Fargo flung himself backward. The glittering blade missed, but not by much. Gaining his feet, he extended the Colt to fire again. This time, he would put a slug through the center of Shem's forehead. But the killer swung the knife once more, and accidentally struck the Colt, nearly tearing it from Fargo's grasp. Before Fargo could firm his hold, Shem was on top of him, thrusting at his throat. Fargo dodged, felt a foot hook his ankle, and the next thing he knew, he was flat on his back.

Shem pounced, slamming his good knee onto Fargo's chest. His knife rang against the Colt's revolver a second time.

The revolver was torn from Fargo's grasp. He twisted as the blade sheared past his jugular, thunking into the earth. Shem immediately hiked his arm to stab again. Balling a fist, Fargo connected with a solid uppercut that rocked Shem but didn't entirely dislodge him. Before Shem could recover, Fargo bucked upward, throwing his attacker off, and scrambled upright.

Shem snarled like a rabid wolf and closed in once more. He moved swiftly for someone with a bullet in one leg, his knife weaving a potentially lethal tapestry.

Fargo skipped to the right. He skipped to the left. He ducked. He twisted. A dozen times he saved himself by only a fraction.

Then Shem blundered. In his eagerness he lunged too far, overextended himself, and stumbled.

Bending, Fargo speared his right hand into his right boot, to the sheath strapped above his ankle. His palm wrapped around the hilt of his Arkansas toothpick, and as Shem straightened, so did he. Fargo met him blade-to-blade. Steel rang on steel.

Cursing, Shem fought all the harder. His knife was bigger, the blade was longer, but try as he might, he couldn't penetrate Fargo's guard. It fueled his fury. Growling like a griz, he feinted low and lanced his knife high.

Fargo barely parried in time. More by accident than design, his blade glanced off Swill's, and the razor-sharp toothpick sliced into the other man's knuckles.

Shem howled and backed off several steps. Blood gushed from the wounds, threatening to render the knife too slippery to hold. With a deft flip, he shifted the weapon to his other hand.

It was the opening Fargo had waited for. Reversing his grip, he threw the toothpick overhand, a feat he practiced almost daily. Usually, his targets were stumps and trees—and he seldom missed.

Shem Swill gaped in amazement at the hilt of the knife protruding from his chest and took several tottering steps. Without thinking of the consequences, he gripped the toothpick and yanked. The knife came out, but so did a crimson fountain. Within moments the front of his shirt and vest were soaked and he collapsed onto his knees. "This can't be!" he croaked, weakening rapidly. "Damn you to hell!"

Fargo was careful not to get too close. "You brought it on yourself," he said, reclaiming the Colt.

Shem tried to lift the toothpick to throw it, but lacked the strength. Blood seeped from both corners of his mouth, and a thin red line trickled from his left nostril. "My kin will finish you," he boasted. "See if they don't!" A fit of coughing afflicted him. "I just wish I could be there to see it."

"You won't." Fargo had half a mind to put a slug into Shem's head, but it would be a waste of lead. The man wouldn't last much longer.

"The high and mighty Trailsman," Shem said in blatant disgust, and predicted, "Clancy and the rest will whittle you down to size." He swayed, his eyelids fluttering, and tried to raise a hand to his chest but couldn't.

"If they're smart, this will end it," Fargo said.

Shem snorted, causing more blood to pour from his nose. "That shows how much you know. The Swills never forget a slight or a hurt. And we never let them go unpaid. You can count the number of days you have left to live on one hand." Shem attempted to say more, but a violent convulsion seized him and he flopped about on the ground like a fish out of water. Another few seconds and he expired with a loud gasp.

Fargo retrieved the Arkansas toothpick. He wiped the blade clean on Shem's vest, then replaced it in its ankle sheath. About to rise, he had an urge to go through Shem's pockets. He didn't make it a practice to search those he slew, so he couldn't account for where the urge came from. Shem had fourteen dollars and eighty cents on him, as well as a pair of dice and a small gold watch. Not a pocket watch, like most men carried, but a small, slender watch typical of those worn by women.

Fargo went to examine the watch more closely but a groan interrupted him. Shoving it, and the money, into his pocket, he rose and turned.

Wilt Swill was sitting up, his left hand clasped to his right shoulder. Wincing, he glanced up and spotted his brother. Astonishment registered. "Shem!" he blurted. Sheer and utter hatred etched his features as he glowered at Fargo and snapped, "May you rot in hell!"

"I hope you have more sense than he did," Fargo made one last attempt to reason with Wilt. "Tell Clancy and the rest of your brothers to let it be."

"Are you plumb loco?" Wilt half rose but was overcome by torment and sank back down. "There isn't anywhere you can go where you'll be safe. From now until the end of your born days, you'll always be looking over your shoulder, never knowing when one of us will pop out of nowhere and take our revenge."

"Then I guess there's only one thing to do," Fargo said, and pointed the Colt at Wilt's sternum. But he couldn't bring himself to squeeze the trigger. He couldn't bring himself to kill an unarmed man, however much that man deserved it.

Hooves hammered to the south, and into view galloped the Carter boys, their pack animals in tow. They reined to a stop in a cloud of dust, and the youngest, John Carter, declared, "We heard shooting and came as fast as we could!"

"I told you to keep on going," Fargo mentioned.

"Sorry, mister," Jack Carter said. "We just couldn't. We need you. Whether you like it or not, we're sticking by your side until we reach the Snake River. Our sister is more important than hurting your feelings."

Fargo happened to glance at Wilt Swill as Jack spoke, and he was puzzled to note a sly grin spread across Wilt's face. Wilt quickly looked away, and when he turned back toward them, the grin was gone.

John gawked at Shem Swill in stupefied fascination. "You killed him! You actually went and killed that man."

"He was planning to do the same to me," Fargo justified the deed, and felt slightly foolish for doing so. What he did and why he did it was his own affair. He had no cause to justify himself to anyone.

"I've never seen a dead man before," John said.

Fargo had to remember he was dealing with pampered

Easterners who had lived sheltered lives in the lap of luxury.

"In fact, I had never seen anyone shot until yesterday at Les Bois when that boy drew on you and you winged him without half trying. You were incredible!"

It amused Fargo to hear someone who wasn't much over twenty refer to a sixteen-year-old as a "boy." But he wasn't amused by the awestruck gaze of adulation John fixed on him. "Don't make me out to be more than I am."

Wilt Swill struggled to his feet. "Some hero you've got there, brat. He was about to blow out my wick. And me with a clipped wing—and unarmed, to boot."

John Carter look at Fargo. "You wouldn't do that, would you? Shoot an unarmed man?"

"No, I reckon I wouldn't," Fargo said. Shoving the Colt into his holster, he stepped to the pinto and forked its hurricane deck. "Let's light a shuck."

"Hold on, there!" Wilt Swill called out. He was pivoting to the right and the left. "Where in hell is my horse?"

"Halfway to the Canadian border by now, would be my guess," Fargo exaggerated, and reined to the south.

"You can't ride off and leave me afoot! Not without a gun! Not without a canteen or a water skin! It would be the same as shooting me!"

Fargo was conscious of Joe Carter's intense scrutiny. "You can make it if you don't run into a grizzly or any hostiles."

"But you shot me!" Wilt practically screamed. "I could bleed to death! Or die of infection!"

"The bleeding has already stopped," Fargo responded, "and infection won't have time to set in if you walk fast and have the wound treated in Les Bois." He clucked to the Ovaro and moved off at a brisk walk.

Wilt Swill shook his good arm in undiluted fury. "I'm coming after you, mister! As soon as I'm tended to, I'm getting me a horse and a rifle and coming after you! Do you hear me?"

They could hear him in Denver, Fargo thought, and for the time being banished the Swills from his mind. It would take Wilt the better part of a day to walk back. Another day would be spent resting up. It wouldn't be until the third or fourth day that the clan would come after him, and by then he would be well on his way to Oregon.

John Carter cantered up beside the pinto. "Mind if we talk a while?"

"About what?"

"That dead man back there, for starters. You killed him, so shouldn't you have seen to his burial?"

"And deprive the buzzards of a meal?" Fargo wagged a hand at a trio of vultures already circling a couple of hundred feet above them. The winged carrion eaters had an uncanny knack for arriving soon after anyone died. "They have to eat just like we do. The same with coyotes and other scavengers."

"I never thought of it that way," John said. "I suppose when a man has lived out here as long as you have, you see things differently than the rest of us."

"No different than men like Dan Tanager," Fargo said off-handedly. "Or the Sioux or the Blackfeet."

"That's exactly my point. You're accustomed to life out here. To living like the Indians. But my brother and I aren't. We couldn't think like you do if we tried."

"Why would you want to?" Fargo asked. "When this is over, you'll go home to Ohio, and live out the rest of your days in peace and comfort."

"Maybe," John said. "And then again, maybe not. I sort of like this wild country. I'd like to see more of it before we're done. I can always take up practicing law again later."

Fargo couldn't fault him there. When it came to wanderlust, he had a monopoly. His own urge to see more of the world had taken him from the Everglades of Florida to the Pacific Ocean, from sunny Mexico to the frigid Canadian northland. And after all his travels, he still wasn't content to sit still for more than a week or two. He had no hankering to set down roots.

"I wanted to go to Europe last year, but my father

wouldn't hear of it," John mentioned. "He said it could wait until I have a wife and a family. Like he did with us."

"Aren't you a little old to let your father boss you around?"

John grinned self-consciously. "You haven't met my father. It's not easy to say no to him." He sighed. "And I guess it won't hurt me to wait. I've been to Europe once, when I was five. I barely remember it. Jack, he was luckier. He was ten, so he has a lot of wonderful memories." The pack horse he was leading slowed and he jerked on the rope. "I envy you to no end, Mr. Fargo. To be footloose and carefree. To be able to go wherever the wind blows you. That's the life for me."

"It's not as glorious as you make it sound," Fargo sought to disillusion him. "In the summer you roast, in the winter you freeze. There are days at a stretch when you go without food and water. Every minute of the day you must keep your eyes skinned for hostiles. Grizzlies and other meat-eaters are everywhere." He skirted a boulder. "There's a lot to be said for a nice home and a loving family."

John wasn't persuaded. "But you do without. So why can't I? I'm not saying I'd roam forever. Just until I no longer felt the need."

In Fargo's more private moments, he sometimes wondered if he would ever settle down. Odds were he would go on enjoying his life of whiskey, women, and wanderlust until the day he went up against someone a shade faster on the draw, or blundered onto a grizzly that refused to die. He wouldn't be the first. Frontiersmen were notoriously short-lived. Just as the fur trappers had been before them. Someone once estimated that for every one hundred men brave enough to venture into the Rockies after beaver, three made it back out alive.

Fargo had been among the first of a new breed. Not that he had planned it that way. It was simply how his life worked out. The Eastern press dubbed men like him "plainsmen," "scouts," and "frontiersmen," and wrote exaggerated tales of their escapades that the reading public couldn't get enough of. A few had even been written about him.

Those who didn't know any better, like John Carter, might think a frontiersman's life was glamorous, but they were sadly mistaken. More than anything else, it was dangerous. Fargo knew of scores of men just like himself who were no longer around. Their scalps adorned lodges in villages far and wide. Or their bleached bones lay decomposing under the merciless sun.

Despite the daily perils, though, Fargo refused to give up the life he loved. He would rather lose a limb than the freedom to go where he pleased—when he pleased—without being hindered by anyone. The freedom he loved so much.

Suddenly Fargo realized John was saying his name. "What is it?" he demanded more gruffly than he intended.

"I was asking what you would do if you were in my shoes. Would you go to work for your father, or would you be true to your heart and let your craving for adventure guide your steps?"

"Do you know what the difference is between a man and a boy?" Fargo rejoined.

"What does that have to do with anything?" John asked. "Are you saying I'm too young to know what's best for my own good? My father says that a lot, but it's not true."

"I'm saying a man makes his own decisions," Fargo clarified. "A boy asks advice on how to make them."

"Oh. I understand. I need to decide for myself. I shouldn't let my father dictate how I live my life." John frowned. "But it's a lot easier said than done. My father likes to do things his way."

The young man launched into a family history. Fargo listened to how their father had taken a rundown business and turned it into an empire. He learned that although they were always given the best of everything, they rarely got to see their father or spend time together as a family. The senior Carter was always too busy with work, always too engrossed in making the next hundred thousand.

"Our mother wasn't much for togetherness, either," John said. "She'd rather spend her time at her socials and club functions than spend it with us. Yet another reason Jack, Suzanne and I became as close as we are."

Fargo pulled his hat brim lower to shield his eyes from the sun, which was well on its Western descent.

"Frankly, I never did understand why my sister married Tom Maxwell," John rambled on. "They had known each other since they were knee-high to your horse, but she never showed much interest in him until, one day, out of the blue she announced he had proposed and she had accepted." John shook his head. "If I live to be a hundred, I will never understand how women think."

"You, and every other man alive," Fargo said.

John chortled, then sobered and remarked, "I think she did it more to get away from our parents than out of love. They were always a lot stricter on her than they were on Jack and I. She was their little princess and they treated her special."

Spoiled rotten was more like it, Fargo mused, but he kept it to himself.

"If she knew what Maxwell has been up to in Oregon, she would scratch his eyes out," John stated. "You should have seen his face when we walked into the general store he's got going. He was upset we had come. He said Susie is gone and we should learn to accept it, as he has." The younger man's face clouded. "And all the while, he kept looking over at a blonde woman in dry goods, and they'd smile at one another, like lovers do. I wanted to punch him but Jack wouldn't let me."

On and on John Carter talked. About his sister. About a girl he once cared for. About a girl Jack once cared for. About the pet dog he'd had as a boy. About the time he had the measles.

Fargo had seldom been so thankful to pitch camp. He asked John to fetch enough firewood to last the night, and for twenty blessed minutes he enjoyed marvelous quiet. He stripped the Ovaro, kindled a small fire, and fashioned a makeshift spit. Then he took the Henry and roved off among the dry hills and gullies after game. He found rabbit tracks but they were several days old. He also saw where several grouse had taken dirt baths, but the grouse had also long since gone elsewhere.

The sun was a golden sliver on the rim of the world when Fargo came to the crest of a low rise and saw that below him stood a buck and four does. The deer fled, bounding toward a patch of brush, the buck in the lead. Fargo fixed a hasty bead on the slowest doe, held his breath to steady his body and his aim, and fired at a range of forty-five yards. The doe flipped in the air, thrashed a few times, and was done for.

The Carters were seated across the fire from each other, their rifles across their laps, when Fargo walked into camp with the doe across his shoulders. They had filled a coffee pot from a water skin and placed the pot on a flat rock partly in the flames.

John was scribbling in a leather-bound book. "It's my journal," he disclosed when Fargo asked. "I've been keeping a daily record of our travels. Maybe I'll get it published one day."

Jack glanced at Fargo and rolled his eyes skyward as if to suggest his younger brother was a few cards shy of a deck. "Who would read it?" he asked. "No one cares about our little adventures."

"That's where you're wrong," John said, unfazed by the criticism. "The last time I was at the newsstand, I counted over two dozen penny dreadfuls."

Fargo deposited the doe ten yards from the fire and drew the Arkansas toothpick. He poured some scalding hot water onto the blade before applying it to the doe's belly. In short order he had her skinned, and had suspended a haunch over the flames. The delicious odor made his mouth water. His stomach rumbled, a reminder that he hadn't eaten since the day before.

While the meat roasted, Fargo scooped out a shallow hole and buried the entrails and other remains to discourage bears and wolves from paying them a visit. The rest of the meat he wrapped in the doe's hide to cook the next day.

"You're a handy gentleman to have around," Jack paid him a compliment as he hunkered by the spit. "Most evenings we make do with beans. We're not very skilled at hunting."

"Our father would never take us with him when we were young," John explained. "We asked a few times, but he always had an excuse not to."

"Some men like to hunt, some don't," Fargo remarked. Those who didn't were usually too squeamish or too lazy to hunt their own food. If it weren't for butchers, markets, and restaurants, they would starve. Civilization was a refuge for those unable to make do on their own.

"I can't wait until we reach the river tomorrow," Jack said excitedly. "Every time we go there I keep hoping we'll find something the rest missed."

Fargo looked at each of their hopeful faces. "What will you do if we don't find anything?" he bluntly asked. It was time they faced up to the truth they had been denying for so long. They could criticize Tanager and Maxwell all they wanted, but they were clutching at the thinnest of straws.

Jack answered. "We'll have to pack it in and go home. I hate to give up, but if Susie is gone, she's gone, and we'll have to deal with her loss as best we're able."

"How can you say that?" John demanded. "We both know she's still alive. We can feel it in our bones. I'll never give up on her so long as I draw breath."

"Ever heard of wishful thinking?" Fargo asked.

John's face pinched in stubborn denial. "Sure, I've heard of it. Don't treat me like I'm some kid. But I'm telling you she *is* alive somewhere." Suddenly rising, he stalked off toward the horses.

Jack leaned forward and whispered. "You'll have to forgive my brother. He's a bit of a hothead."

"Out here that can get a man killed," Fargo observed. He said no more on the subject the rest of the night.

They would learn the hard way, if need be, but they would learn.

John returned after a while and sat off to one side, sulking. His mood lightened somewhat when the meat was done, and he ate as hungrily as his brother.

About ten o'clock Fargo decided to turn in and asked the Carters which of them wanted to take first watch.

"Stand guard, you mean?" Jack asked in surprise. "Is that really necessary? We've never done it before."

It took a moment for the full implication to sink in. Genuinely stunned, Fargo paused in the act of polishing off his fourth cup of coffee. "The two of you came all this way from Ohio, traveled clear across the prairie and the mountains, went on to Oregon and back again, and neither of you ever once stood guard at night?"

"Should we have?" Jack asked. "We honestly didn't think it was necessary. We never saw any Indians. And the only bear we ever saw was a black bear, and it was far off."

"The two of you should take up gambling," Fargo said with a grin. They had more luck than a hundred men. It was rare for anyone to cover as much territory as they had and not encounter some sort of trouble along the way. Even large wagon trains weren't immune. The disappearance of their sister was proof of that.

Jack agreed to take a three-hour watch. John would stand guard next, and Fargo last. Fargo unrolled his bedroll and spread out his blankets. For a pillow, he had his saddle. Lying on his back with his fingers entwined behind his head, he reveled in the celestial spectacle overhead. Twice he saw the fiery streaks of meteors. Finally, sleep claimed him. But it seemed as if he had been asleep only five minutes when he felt a hand on his shoulder, shaking him. "My turn already?" he asked, sitting up.

"You have another hour yet," John said. He was holding a nickel-plated, short-barreled Remington revolver, and he had it cocked.

"What's with the artillery?"

"We have visitors," John said, and nodded at the encircling darkness.

Fargo looked, and beheld dozens of reddish eyes blazing at them from all sides like the eyes of disembodied demons. Throwing his blanket off, he rose and lowered his right hand to his Colt.

"They appeared out of nowhere," John informed him. "I never heard them come up. One second they weren't there, the next they were." He anxiously licked his lips. "What are they, anyhow?"

"Wolves," Fargo said. "Lots and lots of wolves."

5

John Carter snapped his rifle to his shoulder to fire.

"Don't!" Fargo commanded. Grabbing the barrel, he tilted the muzzle at the ground. "Don't shoot unless they attack." Which was highly unlikely. Normally, wolves posed little danger unless they were starved. Highly intelligent and innately curious, they often came close to campfires. But Fargo knew of only a handful of incidents in which they had gone after humans, and then only when the wolves were desperate for food.

"But there are so many!" John declared. "We should drop one or two so the rest will run off."

"It might anger them into attacking, instead," Fargo said. And there had to be twenty-five to thirty out there. Large packs weren't all that uncommon. It was fortunate the wolves weren't hostiles, Fargo reflected. Working in concert, the wolves easily brought down deer and elk. Once, he'd seen a pack drag down an old bull moose.

John nervously licked his lips. "I hope you know what you're doing."

The other brother hadn't stirred. Jack was blissfully sleeping through the whole thing.

One of the larger wolves padded toward them slowly and halted at the edge of the firelight. It had a thick, dark coat, and a long, bushy tail. Raising its nose into the wind, it sniffed loudly several times, then uttered a low yip. At the signal, the entire pack turned and trotted off into the night.

"Thank goodness," John exclaimed. "I thought for sure they would eat us alive."

"Most wild animals fight shy of humans," Fargo said. There were exceptions. Grizzlies, for instance. The massive lords of the mountains weren't scared of anything, including two-legged invaders of their territory. Mountain lions would kill, but they weren't as bold as bears. They preferred to slink up close and jump prey from behind. In contrast, a griz would come right at a person.

"Sorry I woke you," John said. "There's still another half an hour to go before it's your turn to stand guard."

"You did the right thing," Fargo responded. Alone, John might have shot at them, and the wolves might have swarmed the camp before he could get out from under his blanket. "Go ahead and turn in. I'll take over."

"Are you sure? I don't mind staying up longer."

"I'm sure." Fargo wouldn't be able to get right back to sleep anyway. And another ten or fifteen minutes of shut-eye wouldn't make much of a difference.

John moved to his bedding. "Fair enough. I made a new pot of coffee. Feel free to help yourself."

Fargo did just that, and his first swallow made his mouth pucker. The greenhorn had added enough sugar to gag a horse. Sugar was a rare treat on the frontier and most used it in moderation. Fargo took a few small sips, then poured a third of the pot onto the ground and refilled it with water from the water skin. He set the pot on the fire, and when the brew was boiling, he refilled his cup. Now it was a lot better.

The rest of the night proved uneventful. A cougar screeched to the northeast and a roving bear grunted a few times, but neither came close to camp.

By sunrise, Fargo had the Carters up and fed and in the saddle. They ate leftover venison. Jack offered to cook flapjacks but Fargo didn't believe in letting meat go to waste. When a man shot an animal for food, he had an obligation to eat as much of it as he could before the meat spoiled.

The air had a nice, crisp edge to it. Fargo breathed

deep as they rode off. Early morning was one of his favorite times of the day. The world was always fresh and new, and it felt good to be alive.

By noon the arid ground had given way to grass and weeds and brush. Trees sprouted, and toward the middle of the afternoon Fargo spied a line of cottonwoods, a clue that the river wasn't far off.

The Snake River wasn't especially wide, but it was swift-flowing in spots. More importantly, it was a godsend for emigrants flocking West. The Oregon Trail paralleled the river for mile after mile, just as it had followed the course of the North Platte River back on the prairie, and as it would parallel the Columbia River later on. Without those three rivers, the route west would be infinitely harder, to say nothing of being infinitely drier, and many more untold thousands would perish along the way.

Fargo wasn't like most whites. He seldom worried about dying of thirst. He knew the location and course of every river and most major streams between the Mississippi and the Pacific. He was also highly adept at finding water in new, unexplored territory. Yet another reason he was so highly regarded as a scout and guide.

The Carter boys became increasingly more excited the closer they drew to the Snake. After another quarter mile, they lashed their mounts into a gallop and barreled off through the trees.

Fargo came close behind. Presently, he beheld the river. He brought the Ovaro to the water's edge and allowed the stallion to slake its thirst while he dismounted to stretch his legs.

The Carters were still in the saddle. Jack rose in the stirrups and pointed to the northwest. "If I'm right, the exact spot is a few miles in that direction. Let's hurry."

Removing his hat, Fargo upended it and filled the crown with water. "We'll take it nice and easy," he recommended.

"But we can't wait to show you the spot!" Jack said. "We're not tired or hungry, if that's what you're thinking."

"I'm thinking of the horses," Fargo set him straight.

54

"We've been prodding them hard since we left Les Bois. We'll go easy for their sakes, not for yours." Pouring out the water, he placed his hat back on his head and experienced tingling cool wetness clear down to his neck. It wouldn't last long, but the respite from the heat was welcome.

The Carters impatiently waited as Fargo climbed on the pinto, and they were quick to head off again. Out on the Snake River some ducks were feeding. Twice they spooked deer that had emerged from hiding to get a drink. Squirrels chattered at them from high in the trees, and a long brown snake went gliding by at one point, within a few yards of shore.

A rutted track bordered the river, sometimes close to it, at other times a stone's-throw off. The ruts were the result of thousands of wagon wheels digging deep into the soil. Intermixed with the ruts were countless hoof prints left by countless oxen, horses, and mules. The Oregon Trial stood out like the proverbial sore thumb.

John squirmed and fidgeted as if he had ants in his britches. He wasn't pleased by their slow pace one whit.

Then a bend appeared, and both Carters whooped and raced on ahead, Jack bawling, "We're almost there! We're almost there!"

Fargo took his time. When he rounded a finger of woodland, he saw the brothers had hopped off their mounts and were anxiously awaiting his arrival. "This is where your sister vanished?"

Jack nodded and removed a slip of paper from a jacket pocket. "See for yourself. Mr. Tanager drew us a sketch and everything matches. This has to be the right place."

Sliding down, Fargo took the paper and confirmed it for himself. The scout wasn't much of an artist but he had done a passable job, and in his sketch he had listed three landmarks. The first was a gravel bar that jutted thirty feet into the Snake. The second was a low hill directly across the river from the gravel bar. The third, and the one that climbed it for Fargo, was a lightning-scarred tree seventy yards past the gravel bar but plainly visible from where they stood.

"Were we right?" John asked.

Nodding, Fargo surveyed the shoreline. Extremely heavy undergrowth grew to the very brink of the river-bank, part of a tract seven or eight acres in extent. The Oregon Trail came within forty yards of the river, and a path had been cleared down to the gravel bar. The water around the bar was shallow, no more than two or three feet deep, and was almost still. It was an ideal spot for washing clothes and refilling canteens.

A small *X* on the paper marked the spot where Suzanne Maxwell had been standing when she was last seen. It was close to a low bank, within a couple of feet of the vegetation. Fargo could easily imagine a bear or a mountain lion taking her unaware. She must have had her back to the undergrowth and never known what had jumped her. "How many other women were with her that day, did you say?"

"Fourteen," Jack answered. "And one fellow keeping watch. There." He pointed at a log about eight yards to the south. "Tanager told us it was an older man from Connecticut. We weren't able to find him and speak to him in person, but he had sat down to smoke a pipe. It wasn't until one of the ladies yelled that he realized Susie was missing."

Fargo stood in the exact spot marked by the *X*. Suzanne Maxwell had been less than an arm's-reach from a dense thicket. He envisioned that day in his mind; the women jabbering and laughing, and no doubt making a lot of noise as they dipped their clothes in the river and wrung the garments out; the old man over on the log, puffing on his pipe and not really paying a lot of attention. Yes, a bear or a mountain lion were logical culprits. And yet . . .

The gravel bar was only thirty feet long and about six feet wide. The women couldn't have been spaced all that far apart. And the old man had only been twenty-four feet away. If a grizzly or a black bear were to blame, surely someone would have seen or heard something. Bears were big animals, grizzlies were huge. Often when they attacked, they roared or growled ferociously. At the very least, they made a lot of noise plowing through thick brush, as the bear would have done as it dragged Suzanne Maxwell off. Yet no one heard a thing.

Mountain lions were stealthier, and quicker, but they weren't all that bold. They rarely attacked humans in groups. The noise the women had been making, combined with the proximity of the guard and the alien scent of his tobacco, should have been enough to deter a catamount from attacking.

Then, too, if a cougar had jumped Suzanne Maxwell, it couldn't have dragged her off without leaving some sign to that effect. "Was any blood found?" Fargo asked as he peered into the thicket's depths. "Any bits of your sister's clothing?"

"Not a lick," Jack said.

Again, that was odd. Bears and mountain lions inflicted severe wounds. Fargo gave the sketch back to the older brother and began circling the thicket, his eyes to the ground. His curiosity had been piqued. Something wasn't quite right, and he would very much like to get to the bottom of the mystery.

Three months was an eternity in the wild. Any tracks made at the time had long since been erased by the wind and the rain. Fargo had to remember his own advice to the brothers; don't expect a miracle.

"Mr. Tanager claimed he went over this whole area on his hands and knees," John related. "He couldn't understand why he couldn't find anything."

Fargo walked around to the far side of the thicket. Logically, if a predator had dragged the woman off, there should have been paw prints and drag marks where they emerged. Yet there weren't any.

Fargo examined the thicket more closely. If a bear had plowed through it, there should be broken branches and crushed stems. But as near as he could tell, the thicket was untouched. Scratching the back of his head in growing bafflement, Fargo tucked at the knees and studied the thicket low down.

A cougar was a lot smaller than a bear. It would stay low to the ground, dragging Suzanne after it. And sure enough, Fargo found a narrow gap at the bottom where something had gone through. Easing onto his elbows and knees, he handed his hat to John and wormed a few feet into the opening. He saw grouse tracks, recently made. He also discovered a number of odd scrapes that seemed to extend to the other side of the thicket. Crawling in a little farther, he inspected one. It almost looked as if someone had jabbed the blunt edge of a stick into the dirt.

"Anything?" Jack Carter asked as Fargo crawled back out.

"Too soon to tell." Fargo would rather not get their hopes up prematurely. Over the course of the next hour, he crisscrossed the area and traveled hundred of yards up and down the river along the shore.

The Carters pitched camp in a clearing regularly used by the prairie schooners on the trail, and sat next to the fire, anxiously awaiting his judgement. When he walked over, they jumped to their feet wearing apprehensive expressions. "Well?" Jack goaded. "Do you have any idea what happened? Do we give up and head for Ohio to break the bad news to our parents?"

"I'm still working on it," Fargo said. An idea had taken shape but he needed more time to prove it right or wrong. Plenty of daylight was left so, after a hasty cup of Arbuckle's, he resumed his search. John tagged along, but had the good sense not to pester him with a hundred and one questions.

It all boiled down to one question: What could sneak up on a young woman in broad daylight when she was in the company of fourteen other people and spirit her away without anyone being the wiser? Could a grizzly? No. Could a mountain lion? Possibly, although there should have been a lot of blood and pieces from her dress left as evidence.

"I can tell you're stumped," John commented as Fargo returned to the thicket to examine it yet again. "Just like Mr. Tanager and the rest of the people on the wagon train. Just like we were."

"I want you to do something for me," Fargo directed.

"Name it," the young man said.

"Go around to the river and stand exactly where your sister was standing. Pretend you're washing clothes, like she was doing. Splash the water a little. Let me know if you hear me."

"If I hear you?" John repeated, then smiled and nodded. "Oh, I get it. Sure thing."

Fargo dropped onto his stomach and crawled into the low opening. Along much of that stretch, the Snake was hemmed by bluffs or treacherous rocks. It was ironic Suzanne Maxwell had vanished at one of the few spots where it was possible for women to bathe or do their laundry.

A sudden thought struck Fargo and he stopped cold. What if it was more than ironic? What if it were *deliberate*? He crawled on deeper, and the opening widened considerably. In fact, it was wide enough for two people. He saw one of the strange scrape marks and, on an impulse, deliberately gouged his elbow into the dirt and compared the impressions. His terrible conviction grew.

John had done as instructed. He was on the gravel bar, his back to the thicket, going through the pantomime of washing clothes. He was whistling and otherwise behaving just as Suzanne might have done.

Fargo was almost to the river-end of the thicket when he saw a fist-sized rock lying in deep shadow to his right. Picking it up, he hefted it, and a stray beam of sunlight happened to fall across its pitted surface. A surface stained dark with dried blood. He continued crawling until he was at the edge of the bank. John was only a couple of few feet away, bent over the water, oblivious to his presence. Edging out a little further, he coiled his body, and when John straightened, he clamped his left hand around John's mouth while simultaneously rapping him lightly with the rock and hauling backward. He struck so swiftly, he had pulled John a third of the way into the thicket before the younger man galvanized to life and began to resist.

"Calm down. I'm done," Fargo said, and let go. "Crawl back to the gravel bar." Once they were out and on their feet, he thoughtfully brushed dirt from his buckskins.

John rubbed his head and asked, "Why did you pretend to bean me with that rock?"

"I needed to test an idea," Fargo said. "Now we know what happened to your sister."

"We do?" This from Jack, who had witnessed the whole thing from the nearby footpath. He came down onto the gravel bar. "Don't keep us in suspense. If you truly know, tell us!"

"Yes, tell us!" John echoed.

Fargo gave it to them straight, and tossed the rock to the oldest brother. "Your sister was abducted."

Jack examined the rock, his face acquiring the hue of a beet. "Is this what I think it is?" He tapped the blood.

Fargo nodded. "Suzanne was knocked out and dragged off through the thicket. It happened so fast she had no time to cry out. Once on the other side, her abductor either carried her off or threw her onto a horse and snuck off before the alarm was given."

John brought up the obvious flaw. "But if that were the case, why didn't Tanager or anyone else from the wagon train find tracks?"

"Because there weren't any to find. I suspect the kidnapper used an old Indian trick," Fargo enlightened them. "He bundled his feet in thick hides. The hooves of his horse, too, if he had one with him. All there would have been were a few scuff marks. Marks the searchers wiped out when they tramped all over looking for her."

"So an Indian did it!" John exclaimed. "One of those Shoshones, I bet! Or a skulking Blackfoot!"

"The Shoshones have never harmed a white man, to my recollection," Fargo said. "And we're too far West for the Blackfeet." He paused. "I didn't say an Indian was to blame. I said someone used an Indian *trick*."

"So you're claiming the kidnapper was white?" Jack asked in rising horror.

"That would be my guess, yes." Fargo walked midway out on the gravel bar and surveyed the surrounding countryside for as far as the eye could see. "If this were

Apache country, I'd blame them. Apaches are as devious as can be. But the Blackfeet are more interested in stealing horses than women. The Piegans and Bloods think white women are weak and make poor wives. They couldn't be bothered." To the north was a ridge that overlooked the river. From up there a man could keep a close watch on any wagon train passing through.

"But white men don't go around kidnapping women," John argued.

"Not where you come from, maybe," Fargo said, "but out here it's different. These mountains draw outlaws and cutthroats like a dead buffalo draws flies." He nodded at the thicket. "Whoever did it had the whole thing planned out. They knew wagon trains stop here. They knew women like to wash clothes on the gravel bar."

"Diabolical!" Jack said.

"That's not all. That hole in the bottom of the thicket was cut out a long time ago and the limbs carefully removed. A rock was placed in there so the kidnapper would always have one handy to use when he needed it."

"Do you realize what you're saying?" Jack asked. "That maybe other women from other trains have been taken?"

Fargo slowly nodded. He remembered talking to a clerk at Fort Bridger six or seven months ago. The man had mentioned the disappearance of a young woman from a wagon train last Fall. She had gone to the river to bathe, and it was assumed she had been swept away by the current and drowned. Such mishaps were all too frequent. But the woman's body had never been found.

"Other women?" John said, stupefied by the implication. "That reminds me! When Mr. Tanager and I were talking, he mentioned that a year or so ago he had been guiding a different train and two women went off to collect berries and were never seen again."

"Where did it happen?" Fargo wanted to learn.

"He didn't say. Just that it was north of here, so he didn't think they were related in any way."

That made four women, Fargo mused. Four he knew of. There might be more. Dozens of trains traveled West each year, and had been doing so for over a decade. Depending on how long the kidnappers had been at it, the final tally could be a lot higher.

John was turning from north to south and back again. "If you're right, where do we start to look? Susie could be anywhere."

Unbidden, Fargo remembered the card game in Les Bois. How Gus Swill had acted when he joked about the shortage of women in those parts. How Gus had nearly thrown lead at the saloon owner when Barnes made a crack about Gus knowing "all about women." Was he reading more into it than he should? Or could there be a connection? "The best place to start is the nearest settlement."

"That would be Les Bois," Jack Carter said. "But the only woman there was Mabel."

The sun was resting on the lip of the world, giving Fargo an excuse to suggest they cook supper. He led the brothers back to camp and unwrapped the deer meat. While Jack stripped the pack horses and John gathered more firewood, Fargo rigged a spit and impaled chunks of venison on it. He had a lot to ponder. Foremost was whether to ride all the way back to Les Bois on the slim chance his suspicion was valid. There could be any number of reasons why Gus Swill and the others acted so strangely when the subject of women was brought up. To leap to the conclusion they were to blame for the missing women was absurd.

And yet, Fargo couldn't shake the nagging feeling that it deserved to be looked into. He didn't know the Swills all that well, but he had met a lot of other men just like them. Men who thought they had the God-given right to ride roughshod over anyone and everyone. Men who lived by their wits and their guns and weren't too choosy about how they earned their upkeep. Men who, in short, were capable of anything. Including abducting women, if they were so inclined.

It would delay his arrival in Oregon, Fargo reflected. But what were four or five days compared to the lives of the four missing women? Or more? He had enough money to tide him over, thanks to the Carters. Why not see it through?

By the time the meat was cooked, Fargo had made up his mind. But now he had another problem. He would rather travel to Les Bois alone. The Carters would be more of a hindrance than a help. If they suspected he blamed the Swills, there was no telling what kind of trouble they would get themselves into.

"You've been awful quiet," Jack commented as Fargo handed out sizzling steaks on plates from their pack.

"I'd like for the two of you to ride to Fort Hall tomorrow," Fargo informed them. A former military post, and before that a Hudson's Bay outpost, Fort Hall was approximately two hundred miles to the east.

"What on earth for?" Jack responded. "We stayed the night there once. All we saw were a few old trappers and mountain men."

"The wagon trains stop there often," Fargo said. "Find out if anyone has heard anything about missing women." Word spread fast on the frontier. The latest news and gossip were as sought after as gold and silver.

John went to bite into his meat, and glanced up. "What about you? What will you be doing while we're gone?"

Jack dismissed the question with a wave of his hand. "Mr. Fargo's obligation to us is ended, little brother. He did what we wanted. We've learned what we need to know. Now he's free to go his own way."

"But how can he ride off and leave us?" John rebutted. "We need his help now more than ever. Our sister's life is at stake."

"Do you think I don't know that?" Jack said testily. "But you hit the nail on the head. She's our sister, not his. Finding her is our responsibility."

John angrily bit into the venison, then bitterly asked with his mouth crammed with meat, "What kind of man abandons a lady in need?"

Fargo grinned at how they were talking about him as if he weren't even there. "Who says I am?" he challenged. For their own benefit he didn't go into detail. "We'll meet here in a couple of weeks to—" Fargo stopped. He had heard a faint sound. So had the Ovaro. Its ears were pricked and it was staring off into the darkness. Something was out there. Or, rather, someone. For the next instant Fargo heard the sound repeated, and this time he identified it for what it was; the rasp of a cartridge being levered into a chamber. Without a moment's delay he hurled himself across the fire at the two brothers, shouting, "Get down!"

Out of the night poured a ragged volley of rifle fire.

6

Skye Fargo wasn't expecting an ambush. There had been no sign of hostiles in the area, and it would be days before the Swill clan could show up. Or so he believed. But as he crashed into the Carter brothers and bore them to the ground, a fierce whoop pealed above the booming gunfire.

"That's it, boys!" Gus Swill bawled. "Keep pouring lead into 'em! We want all three pushing up grass."

Fargo rolled clear of the Carters and whipped out his Colt. Dirt geysers were erupting on all sides and the air sizzled to the buzz of leaden hornets. "Stay low and follow me!" Fargo shouted. A rifle boomed to the left and he fired at the muzzle flash. Another cracked to the right and he fanned the Colt's hammer twice in answer.

"Gib is down!" someone hollered.

"Take cover, you jackasses!" Clancy Swill yelled. "And take time to aim! Make every shot count! These coyotes have to pay for Shem!"

Fargo heaved up into a crouch and darted toward the vegetation. They had to get out of the firelight. The only thing that had saved them so far was the fact the Swills and their friends were rushing their shots. By his reckoning, seven or eight men were out there, ranged in a semicircle north of the camp.

Jack and John had drawn their revolvers and were banging away. They started after Fargo but they had only gone a couple of steps when Jack clutched at his side and staggered. "I'm hit!" he cried.

Stopping in midstride, Fargo whirled and snatched Jack's nickel-plated pistol from Jack's hand. "Get him out of here!" he bellowed at John. "I'll cover you!"

The bushwackers' rifles thundered nonstop. Fargo felt a slug nip at the whangs on his buckskin shirt. Another creased his hat. He cut loose with ambidextrous skill, firing at gun flashes as fast as they appeared, all the while backpedaling after the brothers. A few more yards and darkness swallowed them. Several last shots were thrown their way, and then the din ceased.

An unnatural stillness prevailed.

John stopped and cradled his older brother close to his chest. "Jack's hurt bad! He has blood all over him."

"Keep quiet and stay still," Fargo directed. They couldn't tend to Jack just yet. Placing Jack's Remington on the ground, he rapidly reloaded his Colt. Furtive movement and whispers wafted from across the way. He spied a shadowy form moving to the northwest, a black blotch against the canopy of sky and stars, and he stroked the trigger. Whoever it was dropped flat with a loud yelp.

"Please," John whispered. "We have to do something! I think my brother is dying!"

Fargo sympathized, but if they moved or made too much nosie, another deadly hailstorm would be unleashed in their direction. And that wasn't Fargo's only worry. The Ovaro and the rest of the horses were picketed twenty feet from the fire. It might occur to the Swills to kill the animals and leave him and the Carters stranded. "Stay with your brother," Fargo directed. He had something to do.

Sidling to the right, Fargo intended to circle around and whisk the horses out of there. But he had only gone a few feet when hooves drummed to the northwest. It sounded like the Swills were leaving, but Fargo refused to believe it. It could be a trick, a ruse to lure him into the open and gun him down. He kept circling until he was north of the fire. No new sounds reached his ears. Nor did he detect movement. It certainly seemed as if the killers were gone. But he wasn't taking anything for granted.

Minutes dragged by. Fargo crept farther from the fire, his finger curled around the trigger. He was staring off into the dark and didn't see a figure sprawled in the grass until he was almost on top of it. In pure reflex he sprang to one side and leveled the Colt, but the figure didn't move or fire. It didn't do anything but lie there.

Warily, Fargo edged closer, hooked the toe of his right boot under the prone shape, and flipped it over. It was the man called Gib, one of Gus Swill's pards. Two shots had cored him above his heart. He was quite dead.

Suddenly a sound brought Fargo around in a blur. John Carter was carrying his brother toward the fire, oblivious to the risk. Tears streaked his cheeks and his lower lip was quivering. Jack lay as limp as an empty sack, arms and legs dangling.

Fargo braced for the blast of rifles, but none came. The younger brother reached the campfire and gently lowered the older to the ground. Jack's eyes were closed and his face was ungodly pale. His shirt was soaked red.

"Mr. Fargo?" John called out. "I think they're gone! What do we do about my brother? Help me, please."

The short hairs at the nape of his neck prickling, Fargo moved into the firelight. He went straight to his saddle, yanked the Henry from its scabbard, and tossed it at John. "Stand guard over by the horses while I examine him."

"Why can't I—?" John began, but stopped at a sharp look. "All right. But we need to do something, and we need to do it right away."

One peek under Jack Carter's shirt and Fargo knew he was beyond help. A heavy-caliber slug had penetrated low on Jack's back, to the left of the spine, and burst out through his abdomen an inch to the right of his navel, leaving a horrible exit wound. A major artery or vein had been severed. So much blood had already been spilled, Jack was lucky if he had a pint left in his body.

"Well?" John hollered from near the string. "How serious is it?"

Fargo sadly shook his head.

The younger man forgot about watching over the horses and dashed back to his brother's side. "There has to be *something* we can do! We have a medical kit in our supplies. You can stitch him up and we'll nurse him until he mends."

"Sewing him up won't do any good," Fargo said softly.

"You can't say that for sure!" John snapped, and frantically darted to the packs. He tore at one like a madman, undoing the leather straps. Flinging it open, he shoved an arm inside, clear to his elbow. "I know it's here somewhere!"

Fargo's blankets were only a step away. Snagging one, he bundled it up and eased it under Jack's head. Jack's eyelids fluttered and his eyes opened, but they were dull and unfocused.

"Mr. Fargo, is that you?" he croaked.

"Yes."

"I feel so terribly weak. Where's my brother?" Jack sluggishly moved his head from side to side. "What happened to the fellows who were shooting at us? And why did you put out the fire? It's so dark I can hardly see a thing."

Fargo glanced at the flames, mere spitting distance from where Jack lay. "The Swills ran off after we killed one of their friends. They might come back, so we shouldn't stay here too long." But they weren't going anywhere with Jack in the condition he was. The slightest jostle would hasten the inevitable.

Jack attempted to rise onto his elbows but couldn't. Gasping, he collapsed and said, "I feel so light-headed. Everything is spinning around." His hand rose, groping, and his fingers limply grasped Fargo's arm. "Be honest with me. How bad off am I?"

"You won't live out the night," Fargo whispered. In truth, it would be remarkable if he lived out the hour.

"Oh God." Jack closed his eyes and shuddered, then opened them again. "I need a favor of you. I know we've asked too much already. But I beg you to take pity on us and help my brother make it home safely."

John was still tearing through the packs like a man possessed. Over and over he repeated, "It has to be here! It has to be here!"

"You've seen how he is," Jack said so quietly, Fargo had to bend lower. "A kid in men's clothes. Easy pickings for the Swills of this world." A convulsion seized him and for a few moments he shook uncontrollably. When the spasm subsided, he sucked in a deep breath and said, "I'm begging you. Give me your word you'll watch over him so I can die easy."

"I'll do what I can," Fargo promised.

"Thank you." Jack feebly smiled and his grip briefly tightened. "I never should have brought him along but my father insisted—" Suddenly he arched his spine, groaned loudly, and exclaimed, "Oh! Oh! I had such plans!"

John stopped rummaging and spun. "Jack? What's the matter?" He raced toward them.

"My sweet sister!" Jack Carter cried. "My poor brother!" And with that, he gave up the ghost. His chest deflated, his chin sagged, and his right hand fell to the earth.

"*Jack!*" John Carter gripped his sibling by the shoulders. Tears poured in a torrent. "Don't die on me! Please don't die on me! I need you! Susie needs you!"

Fargo put a hand on the younger man's arm. "He's gone."

"He can't be!" John railed, and hugged Jack close. "Wake up! I'll get you to Fort Hall! There might be someone there who can help you."

Fargo tried to pry one of John's hands loose, but the distraught young man had his brother in a grip of steel.

"We have to revive him! We need to boil water and bandage him up! You fetch the water while I tear up a blanket." John lowered Jack back down and went to rise.

"Your brother is gone," Fargo stressed, and gripped John by the wrist. "All we can do for him is bury him deep so scavengers won't dig him up again." John tried to pull free, but Fargo held firm. "Listen to me. You're on your own now. The sooner you accept that, the better for both of us."

Slick with tears, John's face contorted in misery. "You don't understand," he said forlornly. "I loved him. He was the best brother a guy could have. Jack always looked out for me. He was always there when I needed him. For Susie and me, both." Breaking down, he doubled over and sobbed.

Fargo rose, picked up the Henry, and respectfully moved off into the darkness so the young man could grieve in peace. He conducted a cautious circuit of the area to confirm the Swills were gone, then dragged Gib's body over close to the fire and covered it with a spare blanket.

John had stopped crying, but was slumped on the ground in despair. He neither moved nor uttered a word as Fargo covered Jack. Since they didn't have a shovel, Fargo roved about under the trees until he found a suitable stout branch with a tapered tip. Kneeling, he jabbed the end of the stick into the ground, twisted, and scooped out a cloud of dirt. It took over twenty minutes to till an area roughly six feet long by five feet wide.

The next step was to find a flat rock over a foot long and use it as a giant scoop. Fargo had been digging for almost an hour when he heard footsteps shuffle toward the hole. He turned, wiping a forearm across his forehead. He had removed his hat and shirt, and his body was caked with sweat.

John sniffled and mustered a brave smile. "You must be tired, Mr. Fargo. How about if I take a turn?"

"You don't have to," Fargo said.

"Yes, I do," John insisted. "He was my brother. I should lend a hand." Stripping off his jacket, he hopped down into the grave. "Why are you making the hole so big?"

"We'll bury both of them together."

"Them?" John said. He glanced toward the fire and

apparently saw the other body for the first time. "Wait a minute. You don't mean him? One of the vermin who tried to murder us?"

"What difference does it make?" Fargo responded. "They're both past caring."

"That's not the point. My brother isn't spending the rest of eternity beside scum." John grabbed hold of the flat rock. "I'll dig a grave just for him, if you don't mind."

Arguing was pointless. Fargo let go, and John scrambled out and stomped half a dozen yards to the south. Squatting, he scraped at the earth with sharp, angry strokes.

"I have a pole you can use to break the soil," Fargo offered, but was ignored. If that was how the young hothead wanted things, it was fine by him. Placing both hands on the rim, he swung up and out and walked over to Gib to go through the dead man's pockets. He found eight dollars and forty cents, a pocket knife, and a thin silver bracelet much too fragile and much too small to be a man's.

Fargo remembered the gold watch he had found on Shem Swill, and took it out. It, too, was more fitting for a lady. He thought of the four missing women and the awful premonition from earlier resurfaced, only stronger. There might be a logical explanation as to why Shem and Gib were walking around with female jewelry, but for the life of him, he couldn't think of one.

Shoving them into his pocket, Fargo dragged Gib to the grave and lowered the body in. He wasn't gentle about it. A hard kick, and the deed was done. Kneeling, he used his hands to shove the pile of dirt he had excavated back into the hole.

John was still digging. Overcome by sorrow, he moved mechanically, every now and then voicing a low sob.

Fargo walked to the fire. He had a decision to make. Since he wouldn't put it past the Swills to sneak back in the dead of night to finish them off, common sense dictated they get out of there while they could. But John wouldn't leave with the grave unfinished. So, after filling his battered tin cup with coffee, he moved off into the dark a dozen yards and sat with the Henry across his legs.

The *thunk-thunk-thunk* of the flat rock biting into the ground was like the beat of a tom-tom. Fargo shut the dirge out and listened instead to the yip of coyotes to the southeast and the screech of a hunting owl much closer at hand. He mulled over how the Swills had caught up so quickly, and the only answer he could think of was Clancy and the rest hadn't been far behind Shem and Wilt. Wilt had put on an act about having to walk back, when in reality Wilt knew all the while his brothers would soon be along.

Time crawled by. The scraping stopped, and John wearily pulled himself out of the new grave. He was exhausted. His jacket and pants were filthy, and he was plastered with dirt. Shambling to Jack, he bent and lifted, but he could only raise the body as high as his knees.

Fargo went over. "Allow me," he said, reaching out.

"No!" John stepped back so abruptly, he nearly fell. "I'll take care of him. Family should bury family." He tottered toward the hole. Depositing Jack close to the edge, John slid down, then reverently lowered his brother the rest of the way. He had to rest a bit before he could climb back out. Uncurling, he clasped his hands in front of him and said, "We should say a few words. A passage from the Good Book would be nice."

"You should do the honors," Fargo said.

John bowed his head. "O Lord God, to whom vengeance belongs, shine forth! Rise up, O Judge of the earth. Render punishment to the proud. Lord, how long will the wicked triumph?" He added, "Not for long if I can help it. Grant me vengeance, God, or grant me death."

Fargo foresaw more trouble brewing. He stooped down to help fill in the grave, but John waved him off.

"I did this much. I'll do the rest."

It was pushing midnight when the young man shuffled to the fire, and squatted, a haunted aspect about him. "I'm the last one," he said bleakly.

"I thought your sister was still alive," Fargo tried to bolster his spirits. "Or so you and your brother kept telling me."

"I thought she was," John said. "Now, I'm not so sure. Maybe Jack and I were tilting at windmills."

"And maybe our notion about whites kidnapping women isn't so far-fetched." Fargo placed the gold watch and the silver bracelet on the ground between them.

John recoiled as if he had been struck. Mouth agape, he scooped up the bracelet and held it to the flames so he could see it better. "Where did you find this?" he gasped. "My mother gave Susie one exactly like it last year!"

Fargo told him, ending with, "My guess is that the Swills are up to their necks in this. I wanted your brother and you out of the way so I could confront them alone, but now we might as well do it together."

"You're damn right we should!" Tears brimmed anew in John's eyes. "I won't rest until I've found my sister and planted every last one of the sons of bitches, just like they planted my brother."

Fargo hadn't been idle while the young man was busy digging. He had loaded the packs onto the pack horses and saddled all their mounts, including Jack's. Now he rose and led the animals over. "We've moving off up the river a mile or so, to be safe."

John was rubbing the bracelet as tenderly as if it were his sister's wrist. "If they haven't returned by now, they never will."

"I didn't ask you to move. I *told* you." Gripping the younger man by the shoulders, Fargo propelled him toward his bay. "I promised your brother I'd look after you, and I'm going to do it whether you like it or not."

Reluctantly, John stepped into the stirrups, then stared morosely at the fresh mound of dirt that marked Jack's resting place. "I'm coming back one day and placing a proper marker on his grave. You wait and see if I don't."

Fargo didn't have the heart to tell him a marker was a waste of time. If the elements didn't destroy it, animals or curious Indians would. Or whites like the Swills, who would shoot it to bits, just for the hell of it. Clucking to the stallion, Fargo rode north along the Snake, the pack horses strung out in his wake.

John followed, slumped in his saddle with his chin hung low.

Fargo pressed on until they came to a bluff that afforded them an unobstructed view of the surrounding countryside, or would have if the sun had been up. "I'll stand guard," he volunteered. "We'll make do without a fire. No need to advertise where we are."

"Whatever you say," John irritably responded. Without bothering to strip the bay or spread out his blankets, he curled up on his side, the bracelet pressed to his chest, and closed his eyes.

Fargo picketed the horses, then prowled the bluff for a while, ensuring that they hadn't been trailed. Sitting with his back to a boulder, he placed his rifle across his lap. He tried to stay awake, but drifted into a fitful sleep. Any noise, however slight, awakened him, and twice he leaped to his feet thinking the Swills were on top of them, but it was only his imagination.

Chirping sparrows heralded a new dawn. Fargo was up before first light and prepared a pot of coffee. He'd need it to get through the day. Breakfast consisted of pemmican from his saddlebags. For once he dawdled. He was in no hurry to rouse John. The young man needed all the rest he could get. Half an hour after sunup, Fargo went over and shook him by the shoulder.

John mumbled a few words and rolled over onto his other side.

The bracelet had fallen in the dust. Fargo wiped if off on his shirt, then shook Carter again. "Rise and shine. The day's a wasting."

As sluggish as a bear roused from hibernation, John slowly sat up and gazed about the bluff in confusion. "Where are we? What's going on?" He saw the bracelet in Fargo's hand. It jarred his memory and he snatched it, crying out, "Not Jack! No! No! No!"

"Would you like some coffee and pemmican?" Fargo

tried to distract him from his grief. "We have a long ride ahead of us."

"I don't know as I'll ever eat again," John lamented.

"You need to keep your strength up or the Swills will do to you as they did to your brother."

Molten fire blazed from John's eyes and he sat up ramrod straight. "The Swills! Thanks for reminding me. I can't give up, not until I've had my revenge." He accepted a piece of pemmican and bit into it with a renewed zest for living.

Fargo got their animals ready to head out. From time to time he checked their back trail for sign of pursuit, but saw none. When he brought the horses over, John was gulping hot coffee as if he couldn't get enough. "Did you save any for me?"

"Half the pot." Grinning, John drained his cup, then stretched and declared, "I feel like I could lick my weight in bobcats."

"That's good, since Gus Swill alone weighs as much as ten of them." Fargo was pleased to see John chomping at the bit, but he was worried John's cockiness would make him careless later on when a single mistake could prove costly.

"Don't fret on my account," John said. "I won't die on you before I've settled with the Swills. On that you have my word." He ambled toward the end of the bluff overlooking the Snake.

Fargo poured himself more coffee and squinted up at the sky. Except for a few puffy clouds, it was as clear as a high country lake and almost as blue. A bald eagle soared above the river, seeking fish. He watched it a while, then glanced southward. The coffee in his mouth suddenly lost its taste.

A line of riders was winding northward along the Oregon Trail. He counted six. Although they were too far off to recognize, he doubted they were innocent pilgrims heading for the Promised Land. Draining his cup, he began kicking dirt at the fire to extinguish it. "John! On your horse!"

When he received no reply, Fargo looked toward the end of the bluff and was startled to discover the younger Carter was nowhere in sight. "John?" Rising, he jogged to the rim. A game trail wound down a rocky slope into a patch of trees below. "John?" he shouted, but again there was no answer. The river was about fifty yards away, rushing swiftly through a narrow gorge. John couldn't hear him above the sound of the rapids.

"Damn." Fargo took the game trail on the fly. The Swills were a mile off, but they were coming on fast. Cupping a hand to his mouth, he yelled at the top of his lungs. "John! Where are you?"

"Over here!"

Fargo sped out of the trees onto a lower slope littered with rocks and boulders of all shapes and sizes. He spotted the younger man out by the river's edge, bent low to cup water into his hand. "Get back here! We need to go!"

John looked up, and smiled. "You should try some. It's cold and delicious."

"We need to go!" Fargo repeated, beckoning.

"Hold your britches," John responded, and leaned lower still. The boulder he had chosen was awash in spray, and either he failed to realize how slick and treacherous it was or he leaned too far, because the next moment he abruptly pitched forward. Yelping, he caught hold with one hand.

Fargo ran, leaping from boulder to boulder, conscious that every second that elapsed brought the Swills that much nearer. "Hold on!"

John was desperately trying to, but his own weight was dragging him lower, toward bubbling white foam.

Fifteen more yards. That was all Fargo had to cover. He streaked around a chest-high boulder and vaulted a small bush. "I'm almost there!"

"For God's sake, hurry!"

What did Carter think he was doing? Fargo wondered. Five more yards and he would be there. Five more yards and he would give the simpleton a tongue-lashing.

John was frantically clinging to the side of the boulder

for all he was worth. It wasn't enough. His left hand began to slip. Frantic, he clawed at the wet surface and got a better grip. It appeared he would be able to keep his purchase until Fargo got there, and all would be well.

Then a white-capped surge of water frothed about him, and John Carter was flung headlong into the river.

7

The Snake River's incredibly swift and potentially deadly waters were well known. More than a few emigrants had died trying to ford it because they failed to appreciate the force generated by thousands of gallons of water rushing along faster than a thoroughbred. The rampaging current swept them off their feet and carried them away before anyone could throw them a line, and either they were never seen again or their bodies were found floating near shore, miles from where they'd blundered.

Skye Fargo had once helped pull a drowned man from the Snake. The simpleton had tried to ride across upriver of a crossing because he was tired of waiting in line for his turn. The wagon boss had warned him that crossings had to be made with the utmost care, but he was confident his horse could make it safely to the other side. In that respect, at least, he was right. The horse did make it—after floundering and unseating its owner, who then met the fate of everyone foolhardy enough to challenge the Snake on its own terms.

Now, as Fargo watched John Carter flung headlong into the churning rapids, he swore a blue streak and whirled, racing flat out for their horses. Carter had one chance and one chance only. To carry it out, Fargo had to outrace the river. The Ovaro might be swift enough, but not leading the pack horses and all the other mounts. In order to save John, Fargo had to leave the extra animals behind. But if he did, the Swills would find them. So be it. He would do what had to be done.

Without breaking stride, Fargo vaulted onto the stallion and reined around. He seized hold of the reins to John's bay and applied his spurs. At a mad gallop he sped to the northwest, paralleling the Snake. Trees and bluffs constantly blocked his view. Then, several hundred yards farther, he spotted a bobbing thatch of hair in the midst of roiling water and heard a piercing wail.

"Help me!"

Fargo galloped around a bend, narrowly avoided a fallen tree, and came to a flat stretch. He also came abreast of John. The current had slowed, but it was still too strong for even the strongest of swimmers to fight.

"Stay afloat!" Fargo yelled. So long as John kept his head above water, there was hope. "I'll throw you a rope up ahead!"

John was flailing his arms and didn't answer.

Thundering around another bend, Fargo flew along another flat stretch of ground. By now the Ovaro had a good fifty yard lead, but it needed more.

Then Fargo came to the top of a rise and saw more rapids several hundred yards beyond—rapids twice as fierce as those John had already gone through. Scores of huge, jagged rocks would tear him to pieces. He wouldn't stand a prayer.

Reining sharply to the left, Fargo guided the pinto down a slope to a six-foot-high drop-off. Springing down, he grabbed his rope and moved to the brink. Quickly, he made a noose and swung the lasso a few times, limbering his arm. The river narrowed somewhat at that point, but unless John was a lot closer to the near side of the river than the far side, the rope wouldn't be long enough.

Fargo held the loop down low, next to his leg. Around the bend bobbed John Carter, still striving mightily to reach shore. "John! I'm over here!" Fargo shouted, but the young man didn't hear him. He hollered again.

There would only be one try. Fargo couldn't miss, or Carter was doomed. He yelled a third time, and finally John stopped pumping his arms and raised his head high out of the water.

"Mr. Fargo! Help me! I can't last much longer!"

Fargo was well aware of that. The cold and the exertion were taking their toll. Eventually John would succumb, were he to live that long; the next rapids would see to it he didn't. Fargo began to swing the rope in practiced circles. "Be ready to catch this!"

Roping a man in moving water was a lot more difficult than roping a stray cow or calf. The noose had to be thrown just right or the current would sweep it out of reach. Fargo locked his gaze on the young man's tousled hair, gauging the distance foot-by-foot, and when he deemed the moment right, he tossed the lasso out over the Snake. It settled a yard in front of John, who lunged, and missed.

Fargo felt a brief sinking sensation. Then, at the very instant the current was about to carry him beyond reach, John lurched forward again and this time he succeeded. Swiftly, he slid the loop over one arm and across his back.

"For the love of God, pull!"

Not quite yet, Fargo figured. Bracing himself, he dug in his soles. The jolt, when it came, was worse than he imagined it would be. The rope went taut and he was yanked forward. For harrowing heartbeats he teetered on the cusp of disaster. Every muscle bulged, every sinew was strained to its limit. Bunching his shoulders, he found purchase and slowly began to move backward. The rope dug into his palms, scraping the skin, and his wrists and elbows felt fit to break, but inch by Herculean inch he moved farther from the drop-off.

The river fought him. It refused to relinquish its hold, the current battering John without cease. Relentless, inexorable, it would not be denied the life it wanted to claim.

Fargo grit his teeth and pulled harder. He didn't like how the rope was scraping against the edge, didn't like how a few of the strands had frayed. Thankfully, John had gone limp, otherwise the task would have been doubly difficult.

Step by slow step, Fargo continued to back up. If only he could pull John in close to shore, where the current wasn't as strong!

"Mr. Fargo!" the young man bawled.

Fargo was concentrating on the rope to the exclusion of all else. Whatever Carter wanted could wait.

"Mr. Fargo! Look, damn it! Look!"

John was pointing toward the bend. A huge log had swept around it and was bearing down on him like a runaway carriage. Foam frothed along its entire length, and the front end bobbed up and down like the obscenely thick neck of a giant snake.

"Pull faster!" John urged.

Fargo was already pulling as fast as he could. He gained another couple of feet, but it wasn't enough. The log was almost there. It would plow into John like a battering ram, and crush his head like an eggshell.

"Hurry!" John screeched, throwing up his arms in a bid to protect himself.

The Snake took pity on them. Just when it seemed a collision was unavoidable, the fickle current caused the log to swerve violently to the left and it missed John Carter by the span of Fargo's hand. Off down the river it sailed, into the maw of the rapids.

Fargo's shoulders were protesting the abuse. But he was almost to the Ovaro. Suddenly turning, he raised the rope and snagged it around the saddle horn. The stallion automatically backed up, as it would do had Fargo roped a steer, and where Fargo's strength had barely been adequate, the big pinto's was more than equal to the occasion.

Within moments, John was clinging to the drop-off. Fargo ran over, bent down, and hauled him the rest of the way out. Removing the rope, he coiled it.

Carter was soaked to the bone. His jacket and shirt were torn, his shoulder holster empty. "Th-th-thank you," he said, his teeth chattering uncontrollably. His complexion was sickly pale, his lips were blue. With every breath he took, his whole body quaked.

Fargo knew the symptoms. A person's body temperature could sink so low that they died. "We have to warm you up," he said, hoisting John to his feet.

John tried to walk, but his body wouldn't cooperate. He stumbled and would have fallen flat had Fargo not caught him.

"Here," Fargo said, and guided him to the bay. John tried to mount up on his own, but couldn't. Cupping his hands, Fargo bent and had him slide a boot into them, then boosted him up.

Grasping the saddle horn, John swayed, but clung fast.

"Try not to fall off." Fargo swung astride the pinto, wrapped the bay's reins around his left hand, and headed for the Oregon Trail. He controlled an impulse to gallop. At the Trail he reined north.

Fargo preferred to put as much distance as he could between themselves and the Swills, but the young man's welfare came first. An isolated stand of trees on a wide bench a quarter of a mile inland from the Snake was as promising a haven as any. When they arrived, he rode into the heart of the stand before dismounting.

John's teeth were chattering worse than before. He was ungodly cold to the touch, and he shook like an aspen leaf in a thunderstorm as Fargo carefully lowered him to the grass.

"Can you hear me?" Fargo asked, but all John did was chatter and groan.

Time was crucial. Fargo hurriedly gathered enough fallen branches for a fire. A dry clump of grass served as kindling. He built the flames a lot higher than he normally would, then gathered his bedroll and Carter's and covered the shivering figure with all four blankets.

What the young man needed now was something hot in his stomach. Fargo emptied his canteen into the coffee pot. It only filled the pot halfway, but that would have to suffice. Their water skin was on one of the pack horses, which by now were in the possession of the Swills. Fargo put the pot on to boil.

John stirred and moved his mouth a few times, but no

words came out. Trying again, he stuttered, "I f-f-feel like I'm b-b-burning up and f-f-freezing at the same time. How can that b-b-be?"

"Be glad you're still breathing," Fargo said. "Just lie there and rest. I'll have coffee ready in a few minutes." Carter's lips weren't as blue as they had been, but he wasn't out of danger yet. Far from it. "It would be best if you shed your clothes so I can hang them over the fire to dry. Can you manage on your own?"

"I'll try." John's arms moved under the blankets. With painstaking slowness he undressed and slid his wet garments toward Fargo.

Fargo placed a handful of pemmican in John's palm. "Chew on these while you're waiting. They'll help."

"I'm not hungry," John said. "All I really want to do right now is sleep."

"Not yet." A sawbones once told Fargo that falling asleep was the worst thing a person could do in a situation like this. "Start chewing."

John frowned, but placed a small morsel in his mouth.

Struck by a thought, Fargo said, "I'll be back in a minute." He took the Henry and moved to the end of the stand to survey the landscape below. The Swills weren't anywhere to be seen, which puzzled him greatly. By rights, the cutthroats should be breathing down their necks. What was keeping them? He'd like to go see, but he couldn't go investigate until John recovered enough to get by on his own for a while.

Fargo returned to the clearing. The aroma told him the coffee was done. Filling his cup, he held it in both hands. It was almost too hot to touch. "Sip this nice and slow," he advised as he hunkered next to his charge.

John's first attempt resulted in a gagging fit. Coughing and sputtering, he curled up into a ball and complained, "Take it away. I don't want any yet."

"Would you rather die?"

"Leave me alone. My eyelids feel as if they weigh a ton." John pulled the blankets up around his ears.

"Fine. If you want to kill yourself, go right ahead,"

Fargo said. "Forget about your sister. Forget what the Swills did to your brother." It had worked once before. Maybe it would work again.

John poked his head out, the old fire in his eyes. "I'll never forget what those bastards have done as long as I live." Trembling, he slowly sat up. "Give me the damn coffee. I'll show you." Impetuously, he took a gulp and yipped like a scalded coyote.

"Sip it," Fargo reiterated.

The piping-hot Arbuckle's soon restored the color to John's cheeks. He was on his third cup, and chomping like a starved horse on his fourth piece of pemmican, when Fargo rose and climbed onto the Ovaro.

"Where are you off to?"

"To see about our pack horses." Fargo didn't go into detail. The young hothead would insist on tagging along, and he was in no condition to tangle with the Swills. "If I'm not back by sunset, as soon as you're able, head for Fort Hall."

"When will you get it through your thick head of yours that I'm not going anywhere until those riffraff have been punished?" John said curtly. "Don't worry about me. I survived the river, I can survive anything. Off you go."

"Have you ever heard the expression, 'too cocky for your own good'?" Fargo asked, and reined to the south. In five minutes he had reached the Oregon Trail. He was making for the bluff where he had left the other horses. A continuous check for tracks revealed that the only fresh ones were theirs.

The bluff reared ahead. Slanting to the east, Fargo rode to the top of a ridge that overlooked it. As he had guessed, the pack horses were gone. So were the Swills. In a roundabout fashion, using every available bit of cover, he gained the top of the bluff and dismounted.

Here, at last, were tracks. The six riders he had seen had indeed found the pack animals. But instead of pushing on in pursuit, they had turned around and gone back the way they came. Why? It wasn't like the Swills to give up so easily.

Fargo went over every square inch of the bluff again,

84

then stood and stared to the south, mystified. Something far off caught his eye. A patch of white, followed by another, then another. Great humped shapes were scuttling across the land in a long row, like giant beetles. Prairie schooners. A wagon train was coming up the Oregon Trail.

At last, the Swills' departure made sense. They had spotted distant smoke from the train's early morning cook fires and either lit out for Les Bois—*or gone after fairer game.*

Mounting, Fargo covered the few miles to the bench at a trot. The wagon train would stop at noon, as they invariably did, and the wagon master needed to be warned about the Swills.

John was squatting by the fire, a blanket over his shoulders, his clothes still hanging on the rope Fargo had strung. "I was beginning to worry. You've been gone quite a while." He smiled and touched his shirt. "They're almost dry. I can ride out whenever you want."

Fargo told him about the emigrants. "If we're right about the Swills," he concluded, "every young woman on that wagon train is in danger."

"Then what are we waiting for?" John quaffed the last of the brew, then dressed. Soon they were once again riding hell-bent for leather along the Oregon Trail, only now they were riding in the opposite direction.

John's good mood faded. He didn't have a thing to say until they crested the bluff and beheld the wagon train nooning two hundred yards below. As was customary, the wagon boss had ordered the sixty wagons drawn up into columns, four abreast. A few cook fires had been lit, but for the most part, few emigrants ate during the midday break. The nooning was mainly for the benefit of their teams. And while the animals rested, friends and acquaintances gathered to enjoy an hour's respite from the toils of the trail.

Sentries were always posted, so Fargo wasn't surprised when a hail rang out and a bearded outrider in homespun clothes and a short-brimmed brown hat rode out to meet them. The man had the look of a farmer, and a friendly manner to match.

"Greetings, friends. Where might you be bound? If it's Fort Hall, you would be well-advised to keep a watch on your scalps. We saw fresh Indian sign not three days ago."

"I'd like to speak to your pilot," Fargo said. Pilot, wagon boss, wagon master—they were all the same.

"That would be Horace Wells. I'll take you to him." The farmer reined his horse around, and they fell into step beside it.

"Tell me," Fargo prompted, "have you seen any other strangers today?"

"Can't say as we have, no," the man answered. "Fact is, we haven't seen any other whites since Fort Hall. This is mighty perilous country to be abroad in. Mr. Wells says that just last year, a husband and his wife fell a bit behind the train he was piloting, and when he went back to check on them, he found the husband dead, his head bashed in."

"What about the wife?" John inquired.

The farmer scratched his bushy beard. "They never did find her, best as I recollect. Mr. Wells says hostiles did it. The poor woman must have been dragged off to live in some buck's lodge."

Fargo had noticed that every time an emigrant or a few horses went missing, hostiles were always blamed. "Wells found Indian sign, did he?"

"I can't rightly say," the man said. "You'd have to ask him."

They passed another outrider and neared the wagons. Curious stares were directed their way. Adults stopped chatting to study them. Children stopped playing to gawk. Having guided a few trains in his time, Fargo knew that any diversion, however minor, was a welcome break in the monotony of their daily grind.

Horace Wells turned out to be a beanpole with the imperious air of an army general. Which wasn't unusual. Wagon bosses generally ruled their trains with an iron will. They were hard men, but they had to be. Hundreds of lives depended on them. Wells was talking to several emigrants and looked around as the sentry rode up. "What have we here, Mr. Simonson?"

Fargo spoke before the farmer could answer. "We're here to warn you to keep a close watch over your women."

"Whatever for?" Wells demanded.

"We believe a gang of cutthroats has been kidnapping women from wagon trains."

A portly emigrant chortled as if the idea were insane. "Kidnapping women? What kind of nonsense are you trying to panhandle? Is this another example of those tall tales frontiersmen love to tell?"

"We're serious, mister," John declared. "Ask Wells, here, about the woman who disappeared from a wagon train he was guiding last year."

"Hostiles took her," Wells said.

"How do you know?" Fargo asked. "Did you find their tracks? Was her husband scalped?"

"No. But who else would have done it?" Wells glanced from Fargo to Carter and back again. "Oh, I understand. You're saying that these phantom kidnappers of yours are to blame? You'll forgive me if I take your outrageous claim with a grain of salt. Do you have any proof of these accusations?"

The portly emigrant had questions of his own. "Who are you gentlemen? How is it you know so much about these alleged abductions?"

"Because my sister was one of the women taken," John said. "My brother and I have been searching for her for months, but he was murdered by the men responsible."

"And who might they be?" Horace Wells asked.

The wagon master was skeptical, and Fargo couldn't blame him. On the face of it, their claim was preposterous. No white man in his right mind would commit such a vile deed. Not when he knew that if he was caught, he would be forced to dance a strangulation jig at the end of a rope.

"As vicious a pack of rabid dogs as ever wore pants," John answered. "Murderers, butchers, thieves, and worse."

As if that were their stage cue, who should come riding in alongside another sentry but Clancy Swill and three of his brothers: Gus, Wilt, and Billy. Gus had a nasty bruise on his jaw from where he had been slugged, while Wilt and Billy both had their right arms in slings.

"It's them!" John cried, and grabbed at his shoulder holster. He forgot he had lost his revolver when he tumbled into the Snake River and his fingers closed on empty air.

"Hold on, there!" Horace Wells bellowed, and at a snap of his fingers, half a dozen burly emigrants ringed John's bay, ready to pull him off.

"But these are the bastards who killed my brother last night!" John cried.

Clancy Swill sat his buckskin as calmly as could be, and chuckled. "What kind of lies has this kid been filling your heads with? I've never set eyes on him before today." He gazed at Fargo and his smile widened. "You two didn't really think you would get away with it, did you, mister?"

Fargo sensed the Swills were up to something. He remembered seeing six riders earlier and wondered where the other two had gotten to. "Get away with what?" he responded. The commotion was drawing emigrants from every which direction, and a crowd was forming.

Clancy faced Horace Wells. "You're the boss here, I gather?"

"That I am," Wells confirmed. "And I'll thank you to explain yourself, sir. Who are you? What is this about?"

"My name is Swill and these are my brothers," Clancy said. "We hail from up Les Bois way, and we're heading for Fort Hall. About ten minutes ago, as we were coming down out of those hills yonder, we saw these two strangers and a couple of others take a pretty young filly off into the trees northeast of here. We were too far off to be sure, but it seemed to us like she didn't want to go. So we came on in to let you know."

Excited whispering and angry muttering broke out.

Horace Wells's imperious features grew harsher. Gesturing at Simonson, he barked, "Pick ten men and conduct a complete sweep of the train. Find out if any of the women are missing."

Simonson began calling out names. The men he chose rapidly fanned out, going from wagon to wagon.

"This is ridiculous!" John snapped, his temper getting the better of him. "We're not the ones abducting women! It's them, I tell you!"

"If that were true, boy," Horace Wells said, "they wouldn't be fool enough to come riding in here like this, now would they?"

"Neither would we," John protested, but he wasn't helping matters much. His anger was antagonizing the wagon master and many of the onlookers.

Fargo had to hand it to Clancy. The scheme was damned clever. It would be his and John's word against that of the four Swills. And while they sat there arguing, the other two riders were whisking a young woman off into the wilds.

Shouts arose on down the wagons. One of the emigrants Simonson had selected was already returning at a run. "Heather Tinsdale is missing!" he roared. "Her pa says she went off to pick some wildflowers and hadn't come back yet!"

Horace Wells barked orders right and left. Men ran to fetch their weapons and horses, and within sixty seconds over two dozen searchers were assembled. "You!" Wells snapped at Clancy Swill. "Show them where you saw the girl last!" He glanced at the rest of the Swills, then at Fargo and John. "Everyone else will be kept under guard until we can get to the bottom of this madness."

"I'm more than happy to help you out," Clancy said, and sneered at Fargo. "Anyone low enough to abduct a woman deserves to have his neck stretched." He trotted off, Simonson and the search part at his heels.

"You're a fool, mister!" John growled at Wells. "You're letting these skunks hoodwink you. That man you just let ride off is a killer!" He raised his reins to go after them.

Wells motioned. Rifles and pistols bristled like the quills on a porcupine, all trained on the young hothead.

"No one is going anywhere, young man," Wells icily informed him.

John had transformed to marble, but his vocal cords still worked just fine. "Damn your stupidity! A woman's life is at stake. Let my friend and me help, or you'll never see her again!

"Was that a threat?" Wells grated through clenched teeth.

Fargo tried to calm John down. "Go easy," he said quietly. "You're only making things worse."

"I'll say what I damn well please!" John fumed. "And I say the Swills are liars!"

Horace Wells slowly nodded. "Someone is lying, that's for sure. And if Heather Tinsdale really is missing, God help whoever is to blame. Because I swear by the Almighty, the guilty party will be hung from the nearest tree."

8

Skye Fargo was all too aware of what the newspapers dubbed a "lynch mentality." When ordinary, decent people became outraged enough, they were capable of deeds as violent and bloody as the crimes that incensed them. Murderers were dragged from jail cells in the middle of the night and hanged. Cattle rustlers were hunted down by regulators and strung up. A sheriff who turned to robbery was hauled kicking and screaming to a pole in the center of a town square and hoisted by the neck to the top.

It didn't take much to incite a crowd to act. So as Clancy Swill led the searchers off toward the trees and the emigrants spread out in a circle to keep anyone from leaving, Fargo sat quietly and debated how best to persuade Horace Wells that Clancy and his brothers were lying.

John, however, couldn't keep quiet even when his life depended on it. With complete disregard for the guns trained on him, he pointed at Gus Swill and declared, "You won't get away with this! Once these people realize they're being played for fools, I'm going to see you pay for murdering my brother."

Gus's dark eyes twinkled with sadistic glee. "I have no idea what you're talking about, sonny. My brothers and me haven't ever killed anybody."

The Ovaro was next to the bay. So when John suddenly grabbed at the stock of the rifle in his saddle scabbard, Fargo bent and gripped the young man's wrist to prevent him from getting them both killed. "Control yourself," he cautioned. "Can't you see he's goading you on purpose?"

"They killed Jack!" John practically wailed, and tried to pull loose.

"And they'll pay, I promise you," Fargo said, holding tight. "But right now it's our own hides we need to worry about."

John scanned the emigrants, and blinked. "Why are they looking at us like that? Are they all idiots, like the pilot?"

Resentful murmurs spread, sparking Fargo to say, "Do us both a favor and keep your mouth shut." John went to speak, but Fargo cut him off and said, "Not a peep!"

Horace Wells turned toward the Ovaro. "I'm glad to see one of you has some sense in his head. Who are you, anyway? You never introduced yourselves."

Fargo told him.

The wagon master's surprise was self-evident. "I've heard about you. Why, the last time I was at Fort Leavenworth, an army major sang your praises to high heaven." Wells's forehead knit and he stared at the Swills with newfound distrust. "This puts things in a whole new light."

Gus had overheard. "Hold on there, mister. Anyone can claim to be someone they're not. How do you know this jasper is the real Fargo?"

"A valid point," Wells conceded. "I don't know any of you personally." To Fargo he said, "Do you have proof of who you are?"

Fargo had to think a moment. There was the letter from the man in the Willamette Valley who had written requesting his help, sent care of a hotel in Denver. But what had he done with it? "I might," he said. Twisting, he opened one of his saddlebags and rifled through its contents.

Gus bent toward his brothers and whispered. Wilt nodded, and Billy eased his left hand to within a couple of inches of his six-shooter. Since being shot, he had adjusted his gunbelt and holster so he could unlimber his revolver in a cross-draw.

Fargo found his other pair of buckskin pants balled up at the bottom of the saddlebag. He had been wearing them the day the desk clerk had given him the letter, and he was sure he had stuck the letter into his pocket. But it wasn't there.

"Well?" Horace Wells impatiently asked.

"I'm still looking." Fargo figured the letter had slipped out and had to be in the saddlebag somewhere.

An emigrant with the body of a bull and a beard down to his stout waist cleared his throat. "He's stalling, Mr. Wells. I don't trust him, or that loud-mouthed boy. Say the word and we'll drag them off their horses and hold them until Simonson and the others get back." Several others voiced their agreement.

John bristled and shook a fist. "I'd like to see you try, you lunkheads!"

Five or six burly emigrants moved toward him, but stopped at a command from the wagon boss. "Enough! I'll decide what is to be done, and I alone. Anyone who disagrees will find himself and his wagon banished from the train."

Just then Fargo located the letter wedged under his boxes of spare ammunition. "Here's the proof you need," he said, pulling it out.

The emigrants were all watching John and him. No one was paying much attention to the Swills, so no one was able to give warning when Gus Swill's Smith and Wesson flashed out and the end of the barrel was pressed against Horace Wells's head.

"If anyone so much as twitches, I'll decorate your wagon boss's clothes with his brains!"

To a man, the pilgrims became as still as statues. They looked expectantly at Wells, waiting for him to tell them what to do. As for the pilot, he was sculpted from granite, his arm lifted toward Fargo and the letter.

"Not one twitch!" Gus emphasized, and nodded at his brothers. Wilt and Billy drew their six-guns and swivelled in different directions. Between the three of them, they had the emigrants covered.

"So the truth comes out," Wells said contemptuously. "Fargo and his young friend were right about you."

"I told Clancy his dumb idea wouldn't work," Gus spat. Gripping the wagon master by the back of his coat, Gus jerked Wells closer to his horse. "Order your people to drop their hardware or I'll make buzzard bait of you."

"I'll do no such thing," Horace Wells responded, and glanced at the man who had wanted to drag Fargo and John from their mounts. "Lafferty, I want you and the other men to shoot these coyotes down."

Lafferty looked as if he had swallowed an apple, whole. "But if we do that, Mr. Wells, he'll kill you."

"Death comes to each of us in our time. If my time is now, so be it. I made my peace with our Maker long ago." Wells squared his shoulders. "At the count of three." He began the count. "One!"

Lafferty and the other men looked at one another. Only a few started to raise their rifles and pistols.

"Two!"

Gus snarled like a beast at bay. "Go ahead and shoot if you want! But know this! My brothers and me won't die easy. We'll take as many of you with us as we can, including women and children!"

The threat gave the emigrants pause. It was no idle bluff. If the Swills went down shooting, plenty of onlookers would die.

"Three!" Horace Wells shouted.

No one fired. One-by-one the emigrants lowered their weapons.

"I'm sorry, sir," Lafferty said contritely. "If you had a wife and children, you would do the same. Please don't hold it against us."

Gus chuckled, his confidence restored. "That's using your noggin, mister. Now have everyone get rid of their artillery, like I told you."

"Mr. Wells?" Lafferty asked.

Horace Wells scowled, but nodded. "Do as they say.

You're right, of course. We can't endanger the women and children on my account."

Billy Swill cackled as rifle after rifle, and pistol after pistol thumped to the ground. "Look at this! These greenhorns will kiss our boots if'n we tell them to."

"Don't push your luck," Horace Wells said.

Gus was savvy enough to know good advice when he heard it. "My sentiments exactly, friend. My brothers and me are riding off, and you're tagging along as our hostage. If any of these farmers and store clerks get any fool ideas, your life won't be worth a pair of crooked dice." Sliding back on his saddle, he said, "Climb up in front of me. No tricks, hear? Or my little brother will gun that lady there with the baby in her arms."

"I surely will!" Billy whooped, and cackled some more.

Fargo was amazed the Swills hadn't ordered him to throw his Colt down. But then, they weren't the brightest candles in the wax factory. He wasn't about to try anything, though, not when Gus's revolver was gouged against the wagon boss's spine and Billy was just itching to fling lead at the emigrants.

Billy and Wilt moved their mounts in on either side of Gus. Together, alert for backshooters, they rode northward at a walk, Billy wearing that wicked smirk of his.

"We can't let them just ride off like that," an emigrant whispered in protest.

"They won't get far," Lafferty predicted. "As soon as they let Mr. Wells go, we'll mount up and chase them down."

But the Swills didn't release Wells. They broke into a gallop, heading in the same direction Clancy had taken the search party, and soon were out of sight over a rise.

"To your horses, men!" Laffery bellowed, and the earlier scene was repeated. Emigrants rushed to their mounts. Saddle blankets and saddles were thrown on as fast as could be managed. And in no time, seventeen more riders were set to depart.

"Mr. Wells said you're a scout, correct?" Lafferty addressed Fargo while keeping a tight rein on his skittish mare. When Fargo nodded, he said, "Then maybe you should lead us. Just don't do anything that will get Mr. Wells killed."

Without another word Fargo took up the chase. From the top of the rise he spotted the Swills going over a hill half a mile away. They were riding like bats out of Hades and raising a dust cloud as thick as fog. He spurred the stallion to a gallop and shot across the intervening lowland. Midway across, in a patch of mesquite and stunted shrubs, he glimpsed a crumpled form and hauled stiffly on the reins. The pinto slid to a stop on its hindquarters, and several of the riders behind him came perilously close to colliding with him.

"What in the world?" Lafferty blurted. "What did you do that for?"

Fargo was out of the saddle and over to the body before most of the emigrants realized it was there. Horace Wells lay on his stomach, one arm flung out, the other under his head as if cushioning it. A red puddle was spreading outward from his neck.

"Dear Lord, no!" Lafferty breathed.

"They didn't!" someone else cried.

But they had. Fargo rolled Wells over. The wagon boss' throat had been slit from ear to ear, the cut deep and clean, his jugular completely severed. His eyes were wide open, and Fargo put a finger to each eyelid and closed them. "Have two men take the body back," he directed.

The emigrants had been shocked into momentary silence. Now their fury surfaced, and they all began talking at once. Some heaped curses on the Swills. Others vented oaths of revenge.

Lafferty picked two to do Fargo's bidding, and off they sped. The rest were a study in steely eyed determination. They were now fully conscious of the type of men they were dealing with, and they were out for blood.

Fargo led them up the hill. On reaching the crest, he was perplexed to see Simonson and the other members of the search party charging toward them like calvary troops charging into battle. Raising an arm, he called out for those with him to halt.

Apparently their arrival was as much of a surprise to Simonson and his bunch. Simonson brought them to a stop and demanded, "What's going on here, Lafferty?" He speared a thick thumb at Fargo and Carter. "We were just told they killed Mr. Wells."

"Who told you a lie like—?" Lafferty started to ask, and swore mightily. "The Swills! *They* murdered Mr. Wells, not these two." He rose in his stirrups and scanned the other group. "Where are they, Abe? Those Snakes must be held to account for their sins."

Simonson twisted in his saddle. "They were right behind us, I thought."

Fargo sighed. The Swills, naturally, were gone, but they couldn't be far ahead. "Send half the men back to the wagon train," he ordered. "The rest of us will push on."

"Hold on, there, mister. Who put you in charge?" Simonson asked. "And why send so many? The more guns, the better. We've got two-thirds of the men from our wagon train along."

"Leaving that many less to protect your families," Fargo said, and trotted on. He imagined the Swills would make a beeline for Les Bois and it was his intention to overtake them well before they got there. Clods of earth that had been churned by Simonson's men guided him to woods to the northeast. It was there that Gus, Billy, and Wilt had caught up to the searchers, and once the emigrants had been duped into racing back, the four Swills had galloped off to the northwest.

Fargo glanced over his shoulder. Simonson had done as he'd suggested and sent half of the men back to the train. Hiking an arm, Fargo led them in pursuit. For over an hour they traversed rugged country that taxed their horses, and their horsemanship. The trail was easy to follow. The Swills were in such a hurry, they left sign a ten-year-old could find.

In time, Fargo came to a clearing. Tracks showed

where the four Swills had met up with the other two members of their party. Other tracks confirmed they had the pack horses. But the prints that interested everyone the most were those of a woman. Fargo pointed them out to the emigrants.

"It must be Heddy Tinsdale," Lafferty said. "They've abducted her, just like you tried to warn us they would."

"That poor, sweet girl," Simonson said. "She must be terrified out of her wits. She's only eighteen."

"Nineteen," corrected a middle-aged man who was nosing his mount up from the rear of the group. He wore sadness like a shroud.

"Mr. Tinsdale!" Lafferty blurted.

"We didn't notice you were along, George," Simonson said. "We're sorry about your daughter. Rest assured we'll do whatever it takes to return her to you and your wife, safe and sound."

Tinsdale faced Fargo. "Be honest with me, sir. Do you think these outlaws will murder her like they did Mr. Wells?"

"I don't know what they do with the women they steal," Fargo admitted, "but I can't see them going to all this trouble if all they aimed to do was kill her."

On into the wilds they pushed, Fargo setting the pace. John Carter and George Tinsdale were silent specters on either side. Hour after tiring hour passed. It was close to three, and they were crossing a grassy valley when a small white object ahead caught Fargo's attention. He reined toward it.

A six-foot-long tree branch had been trimmed of shoots and stuck in the ground where they were bound to see it. The top of the branch had been split, and wedged into the crack was a yellowed sheet of paper.

"What now?" Simonson asked.

Fargo pried the paper from the branch. He read the crudely scrawled note aloud. It was short and to the point. "Stop trailing us you sons of bitches or the girl dies."

Another refrain of oaths greeted the threat. Laffery wagged his rifle and hollered, "They're trying to buffalo us, boys! They won't dare harm Heddy because they know they'll pay, and pay dearly! I say we all push on, and the Swills be damned!"

"Not so fast," Simonson said. "The Swills know they'll hang, no matter what they do, so they might murder Heddy to spite us." He motioned at Heddy's father. "I say we hear what George wants to do. He has more at stake than any of us."

Tinsdale gnawed on his lower lip. He stared at the note, then at the untamed wilderness beyond, and finally at Fargo. "You've impressed me as being a man of honor and intelligence. What do you suggest?"

Fargo hooked a leg across his saddle and leaned an elbow on it. He repaid the compliment by being brutally honest. "We're close. Very close. And the Swills know it. They know we'll catch them soon, which is why they left the note. I wouldn't be surprised if one of them is spying on us right this second."

The statement created a stir, and many of the emigrants raised their rifles and anxiously scoured the vicinity.

"If we keep on, Mr. Tinsdale," Fargo said, "the Swills will carry out their threat, if for no other reason than to give themselves a better chance of escaping. Right now your daughter is riding double with one of them, and his horse is tiring."

"God, no," the father said, profoundly distraught. "She's our only child. It would crush my Harriet's heart. To say nothing of my own."

"So you're advising us to turn around?" Lafferty asked. "What about Heddy? How can we abandon her?"

"I didn't say we should," Fargo corrected him. "We'll head for the wagon train like they want. Make them think they've scared us off. Once we're in the trees, the rest of you will keep going. I'll hide and continue tracking them once I'm sure it's safe."

"You're going on alone?" Simonson said.

"Not on your life, he isn't," John broke in. "Have your forgotten my brother? I'm seeing this through to the end."

"I am, too," Tinsdale said. "What sort of father would I be if I turned my back on my own daughter?"

"Think for a minute," Fargo urged. "If they're spying on us, they might not notice if just one of us slips away from the rest. But they sure as hell will notice if three of us do. And since I'm the only man here who tracks for a living, I'm the one who has to go on."

George Tinsdale removed his hat and ran a hand through his greying hair. Fatherly love wrestled with logic, and logic won. "Very well. As much as it goes against my grain, I'm willing to permit you to carry on alone."

"Well, I'm not," John stated. "I made a vow and I intend to keep it. Where the Swills go, I go, and there's no way anyone can change my mind."

Fargo was becoming tired of the younger man's selfish attitude. "And what about the girl? Her life doesn't mean a thing to you?"

The emigrants stared at John, their disapproval plain. Lafferty voiced the sentiments of the rest when he said, "Be reasonable, youngster. Mr. Tinsdale's daughter matters more than your thirst for vengeance."

"Please, son," Tinsdale pleaded. "For Heddy's sake, if not for mine or anyone else's. I'm terribly sorry about your brother. But getting her killed won't bring him back again, will it?"

John made a growling noise deep in his throat and smacked his right fist against his left palm. "I hate this! I simply hate it!" For a few seconds he regarded the ring of faces with blatant resentment. Then his shoulders slumped and he averted his gaze. "All right. I'll do as you want. But don't expect me to like it."

Fargo slid his left boot into its stirrup. "I'll lead the way back. But three or four of you need to stay close so the Swills won't notice when I break away."

In compact order they wheeled their animals and walked their horses into the trees. They put on a good show. Tinsdale was a portrait of misery. John was mad enough to spit tacks. Many of the others were upset at being thwarted, and it showed.

Fargo had to admit that if he were the Swills, he would think the emigrants had given up all hope.

As soon as the trees closed around them, Tinsdale, Simonson, and Lafferty reined their horses up alongside the Ovaro. Fargo slowed to let them pass, and once they had, he reined around a thicket and on into a cluster of saplings. Doubling over the saddle, he watched the rest of the party go by. John Carter brought up the rear, and he was none too happy. For a moment Fargo thought the hothead would veer aside, too, but John was as good as his word and soon everyone had melted into the distance.

Fargo was alone. He peered out into the valley, but no one appeared. As motionless as the trees around him, he bided his time. The Ovaro was well-trained, and other than an occasional twitch of an ear and flick of its tail, it never moved.

Fargo figured an hour should be long enough. By then, the Swills were bound to be convinced the emigrants were gone, and would be riding hard to the north.

Bit by bit the sun climbed, bit by bit the shadows lengthened. At last Fargo uncurled, lashed the reins, and cantered from concealment. No lead was thrown in his direction. No shouts were raised. His gambit had worked.

On the far side of the valley were more tracks. They revealed that five of the Swills had gone on ahead while one had stayed behind to see if the emigrants heeded the note. When he was convinced they had, the sixth man had ridden off to catch up to his friends and relay the good news.

The Ovaro stallion ate up mile after mile, but Fargo was careful not to gain too much ground. It was best if he caught up to the Swills after the sun went down, when he could use the element of surprise to best advantage.

Fargo hadn't wanted to say anything to John or the emigrants, but he was glad to be on his own. The emigrants were ill-matched against hardened desperadoes like the Swills, and for their own sakes it was better they had been induced to go back.

The same applied to young Carter. A man blinded by

bloodlust took reckless gambles that cooler heads avoided. John's fiery desire for vengeance would only get him killed.

High hills rimmed the horizon. Fargo reached them as the sun was setting, and slowed the pinto to a walk. The Swills would make camp soon and he wanted to come up on them when they were ringed around their campfire and off guard.

Fargo got to thinking about Suzanne Maxwell and the other missing women. Were they alive? Or had the Swills killed them after indulging themselves? Come what may, another visit to Les Bois was in order.

Twilight descended, shrouding the hills in gloom. Fargo wove on until it was too dark to see the tracks he was following. Reining to the left, he climbed a steep slope to a broad shelf. From there he could see quite a distance.

About two miles off, a campfire glimmered. Smiling to himself, Fargo climbed off of the pinto. He would wait a while before moving in. While the stallion nipped grass, he treated himself to a handful of pemmican. He was on his third piece when he was startled by the thud of hooves, from the south.

Fargo pushed erect. Either some of the Swills had somehow swung around behind him, or he was in for an unwanted surprise. Swinging back onto the Ovaro, he descended until he was twenty feet from the bottom. He made little noise, so the pair of riders who trotted out of the darkness had no inkling he was there until he spoke. "I thought the two of you agreed to return to the wagon train."

John Carter and George Tinsdale reined up.

Fargo rode down, anger bubbling within him.

Tinsdale wore a guilty expression, but Carter was defiant, as usual. "I told you I wanted in on this and I meant it," John defended his betrayal of trust. "Before this night is out the Swills will rue the day they were born."

"And you, Tinsdale?" Fargo asked. "What's your excuse?"

"I'm sorry. I can't forsake my daughter in her moment of greatest need. John convinced me to rejoin you." Tinsdale patted his mount. "We've nearly ridden our horses into the ground to catch up. I was beginning to believe we never would." He gazed off across the hills. "Are the kidnappers nearby?"

"Close enough."

John grinned and hefted his rifle. "Good. I can't wait to get them in my sights."

"Just so they don't get you in theirs," Fargo said.

9

The Swills had camped in a gully at the base of a hill, an ideal spot. The gully helped to hide their campfire, and from the top of the hill a lookout could see back down the trail a fair distance thanks to the half-moon that had risen and was bathing the countryside in its pale radiance.

Skye Fargo was too savvy to approach from the direction they expected. He circled around to the far side of the hill, dismounted, and led Carter and Tinsdale toward the top on foot. His hope was to get above the Swills and pick them off like clay targets in a shooting gallery. Sixty feet up he froze.

A cough from higher up confirmed someone was up there keeping watch.

Flattening, Fargo motioned for John and George to do the same. Tinsdale was breathing heavily, more from the excitement than the exertion. He was a farmer by trade, and tangling with cutthroats was new to him. John was eagerly fingering his rifle and clearly couldn't wait to start shooting Swills. Yet he, too, had never killed before. Neither had any business being there, but Fargo wasn't about to waste his breath trying to convince them of that.

"The two of you stay here," Fargo whispered. He had told them before they started out that they must do exactly as he told them, and they had agreed. But since they had already gone against his wishes once, he wouldn't put it past them to do so again. "And I mean *stay*," he emphasized. He crawled on to forestall debate.

A stiff wind out of the northwest helped matters some. It masked the few slight sounds Fargo made as he snaked high enough to spot a squat shape outlined against the stars. It was the silhouette of a seated figure. The lookout.

Sliding his right knee toward his chest, Fargo dipped his fingers into his boot and withdrew the Arkansas toothpick. He left the Henry lying in the grass and resumed crawling with consummate care. It took him ten minutes to cover ten feet. By then he was only a couple of yards from the lookout. He couldn't tell who it was, but he could see the stock of a rifle that lay across the man's legs.

The lookout's arms were moving. He was doing something with his hands.

Fargo inched closer. Suddenly there was a scraping noise and a small flame flared. The lookout had rolled a cigarette and lit it. The glow washed over the lookout's face but blinked out almost at once. Fargo smelled the acrid odor of tobacco and heard a contented sigh. As silently as a ghost, the Trailsman moved higher still.

Fargo had no compunctions about what he was about to do. The Swills had murdered Jack Carter. They had killed Horace Wells. They had abducted Heddy Tinsdale and Suzanne Maxwell and other unsuspecting women. They had to be stopped before they caused more grief and suffering.

Turning them over to the law wasn't practical. For one thing, there *was* no law west of the Mississippi except for an occasional town marshal, and their jurisdictions were limited to the towns they served. County sheriffs didn't exist because there were no counties. For that matter, there were no States. Only immense, uncharted territories where badmen could roam to their heart's content and indulge in all manner of mayhem without fear of having a posse after them.

As for the military, the army was primarily concerned with the safety of emigrants bound for Oregon and California. Patrols were infrequent, and then only established trails. Soldiers weren't meant to do the job of lawmen.

Small wonder, then, ordinary people were forced to take the law into their own hands. Small wonder lynch parties were much too common, and vigilantes served in the place of duly constituted law officers.

Fargo was only eighteen inches from the lookout's broad back. Tensing, he saw the man raise a hand to puff on the cigarette. He waited for the hand to descend again before he struck. Suddenly, behind him, there was a faint scrape, the sound of a foot dragging across the ground.

The lookout instantly spun, the cigarette dangling from a corner of his mouth.

For a span of heartbeats Fargo and the man were eye-to-eye. It wasn't one of the Swills, or at least not one he had previously encountered. Then the man galvanized to life and opened his mouth to shout a warning while snapping the rifle to his shoulder.

Fargo surged upward, clamped his left hand over the lookout's mouth, and thrust with the toothpick. The double-edged blade sliced through the man's wool shirt and buried itself to the hilt between two ribs. Stiffening, the lookout struggled to free himself, but the next second blood spurted from his nose and lips and he sagged, weakening fast.

Fargo stabbed him again, and yet once more, to be sure, and didn't let go until the man stopped twitching. He wiped his left hand on the lookout's shirt, did likewise with the toothpick, and slid the knife into his ankle sheath.

Boiling mad inside, Fargo turned.

John and George Tinsdale had followed him up. John had brought the Henry, and now held it out to him. "What are you waiting for? Let's get this over with."

The young man would never know how close Fargo came to slugging him. They had both nearly gotten him killed. But there wasn't a moment to spare. Snatching the Henry, Fargo dropped onto his belly and peered over the hill.

A small spring glistened on the near side of the gully. Grass covered the bottom, and was being nipped by the horses. Lounging around the fire were Clancy Swill, his brothers Gus, Billy, and Wilt, and Porter, Gus's friend from the card game in Les Bois, the man whose nose Fargo had broken. Huddled between Clancy and Gus was their captive.

Heddy Tinsdale was no girl. At nineteen, she was in the full flower of her beauty. Luxurious russet hair framed a lovely face currently creased in anxiety. She possessed a full, voluptuous body, the kind that turned heads on a city street. Her wrists were bound behind her back, and she was gazing sadly into the fire. But she wasn't devastated by her abduction, as some women would be. Far from it. Now and then she cast spiteful glances at her captors. And when Gus had the audacity to place a hand on her thigh, she suddenly bent and snapped at his fingers with her teeth. Gus jerked back, and Clancy and the others laughed heartily at his expense.

"My poor Heddy," Tinsdale softly groaned, and went to shove to his feet.

"Don't you dare," Fargo whispered, grabbing his arm. "We have to do this right or she might take a slug."

John was awestruck. "She's beautiful!" he whispered. "I can't fault those bastards for their taste in women."

"Temper your urges, young man," Tinsdale said gruffly. "That's my daughter you're talking about."

"No disrespect intended, sir," John said sincerely. "It's just that I haven't seen anyone as lovely as her since I can't remember when."

Fargo focused on the slope. It was bare of cover. Not so much as a single bush grew anywhere. He'd have liked for one of them to move in close to spirit Heddy out of there when the lead started to fly, but doing so would entail working around the hill and coming up on the gully from the side. He glanced at his companions, debating whether to pick one of them for the job. Tinsdale had all the stealth of a cow, and John couldn't be trusted to do as he was instructed. But he couldn't do it himself. He was the best shot, and the top of the hill was the best vantage point.

Clancy Swill had twisted and was gazing upward. From where he sat he couldn't see the body of the lookout, but he could definitely tell the lookout wasn't where he was supposed to be. Cupping a hand to his mouth, he hollered, "Donny, where in hell are you?"

Removing his hat, Fargo jammed the dead man's head-gear onto his own head and sat up. He was banking that in the dark, Clancy couldn't tell the difference, and he waved an arm to signal all was well.

"No falling asleep up there, you hear me?" Clancy yelled. "We don't want anyone sneaking up on us!"

Gus Swill laughed. "That's not likely to happen, big brother. I saw those pilgrims tuck tail and ride away with my own two eyes."

"They're not the only ones we have to worry bout," Clancy said, "or have you forgotten this is Injun country?"

Their voices dropped, and Fargo wasn't able to hear the rest. "One of us needs to sneak down there and be ready to help Heddy," he whispered. "John, you're elected. Don't shoot until I do."

"Why him? She's my daughter," Tinsdale objected louder than he should.

"Keep your voice down, damn it!" Fargo whispered, and explained, "John is younger and quicker and can get her out of there a lot faster than you could."

John beamed, but whether because he was happy to do his part to save Heddy or because he entertained a more personal motive, it was hard to say. "I'm on my way," he said, and scooted back down the hill until he was about midway, then he carefully angled around toward the gully.

"Can we trust him?" Tinsdale whispered the very question that was foremost on Fargo's mind.

"No. But he's all we have."

Clancy and his brothers were passing around a bottle of rotgut. Billy took a long swig and wiped his mouth on his sleeve. Leering suggestively at Heddy, he imitated a crowing rooster, even going so far as to flap his arms in imitation of a rooster's wings. His brothers thought he was hilarious.

"They're animals," Tinsdale whispered. "Filthy, rotten animals. Every last one deserves to be exterminated."

"No argument here," Fargo said. He had been holding the Henry across his knees, but now he tucked the stock to his shoulder. He didn't aim at the Swills. Not yet. Not until John was in position.

"Why did this happen to us?" Tinsdale wondered aloud. "We're decent people. We go to church regularly and we've never harmed a soul. How can God let our daughter fall into the clutches of these degenerates?"

Fargo had no answer. He wasn't a minister. He wouldn't presume to try to guess why bad things happened to good people. Men a lot wiser than him had wrestled with the dilemma and had come up with no clear-cut answer.

"All we wanted is to start a new life in the Promised Land," Tinsdale whispered. "A hundred and sixty acres of free land for every settler, we were told. And the land is supposed to be lush and fertile."

"In some parts it is," Fargo whispered. In other parts, Oregon was as dry as a desert. "You'll like it there." The climate was mild year-round, and there weren't any hostile Indians bent on lifting a man's scalp.

"We needed to leave Pennsylvania," Tinsdale mentioned. "I'm ashamed to admit it, but we were involved in a scandal. There was talk linking our daughter to the son of one of the richest men in Montgomery County."

Fargo had lost sight of John and was trying to locate him again.

"Our Heddy has always been headstrong. She has a will of her own, that one, and no amount of reasoning can change her mind. Once she blossomed out, the men began to take notice. And much to our dismay, she didn't mind one bit. Truth to tell, she liked all the attention."

"Don't tell me you're one of those fathers who can't accept his little girl growing up?" Fargo whispered.

"It's not the growing up I mind. It's how she has been

behaving. Gallivanting around with different men. Staying out to all hours. No proper woman would do such a thing."

"Ever been to Texas, Mr. Tinsdale?" Fargo asked.

"No, I can't say as I have. Why?"

"The cowboys down there have a saying." Fargo thought he saw John moving down below, but it was a trick of the moonlight and shadows.

"What saying?" Tinsdale coaxed.

"That there are two kinds of women in this world. Those who are married, and those who are still alive."

Despite himself, Tinsdale grinned. "Amusing, but hardly pertinent. Most women marry because they want to. Out of love. They still know how to live, only they want someone to do it with."

Now, on the right side of the gully something really did move. It was John, on his hands and knees, slinking toward the tethered horses. He probably assumed he was being clever since the horses hid him from the Swills. But he was making the worst mistake he could. The horses had seen him, and several pricked their ears and snorted.

"Damn," Fargo said. Tossing the dead man's hat behind him, he jammed his own hat back on.

Clancy and Wilt Swill had noticed the animals were acting up and were watching them intently. Wilt rose onto one knee and said something to Billy, who placed his left hand on his revolver.

"What is Carter doing?" Tinsdale whispered. "Doesn't he realize he could ruin everything?"

John was in a crouch now, moving toward the far end of the string. He held his rifle at his waist, ready for use. Despite all his talk about how beautiful Heddy was, John wasn't all that concerned for her safety. He had one thing and one thing only on his mind: revenge.

All hell was about to break loose.

"How good a marksman are you?" Fargo asked as he fixed a bead on Clancy Swill's chest. Clancy was the leader. Kill him, and the rest would panic and be that much easier to pick off.

"Not much of one, I'm afraid," Tinsdale said, sighting down his rifle. "I shot rabbits and squirrels when I was a boy, and I've gone deer hunting a few times, but that's the extent of my experience."

"Aim for the kid with the sling," Fargo said. Billy was most apt to shoot Heddy out of sheer spite.

"I'll try," Tinsdale replied.

The moment Fargo dreaded arrived. John reached the end of the string, but instead of squatting and waiting, he hiked his rifle and charged on around, blasting away like a madman. His first shot blew a hole in Porter's skull the size of an apple. His second missed. And then the Swills were on their feet, returning fire.

Fargo stroked the trigger. Just as he did, Wilt Swill jumped up, directly into his sights. The slug intended for Clancy slammed Wilt between the shoulder blades and pitched him onto his chest.

Tinsdale fired, too, but he missed.

Billy Swill was up off the grass and thumbing shots with remarkable proficiency, shooting at Carter. John's legs flew out from under him and he sprawled onto his side, hit, but he wasn't dead. Twisting, he fired from where he lay.

Fargo tried to set his sights on Clancy again but Clancy was on the move. Bounding behind Heddy, Clancy used her as a shield.

"No!" George Tinsdale bawled, and barreled down the hill to his daughter's rescue. "I won't let her come to harm!" He had only gone a few steps when he cried out, clamped a hand to his ribs, and toppled.

Gus Swill had entered the fray and was peppering the top of the hill. Fargo had to drop below the rim or absorb lead. When he raised his head again, John wasn't moving and the three surviving Swills were backing toward the horses. He snapped off a shot and was repaid with a fusillade. Ducking, he waited for the hailstorm to end. A horse whinnied. Hooves pounded. Daring to look, he glimpsed the Swills fading rapidly into the murk. Heddy was riding double, behind Clancy.

Fargo leaped erect and aimed at Gus Swill's back, but

the Swills were swallowed by the night, and he had no target.

George Tinsdale moaned and endeavored to sit up. He had dropped his rifle and crabbed toward it. "We must stop them! We can't let them take her!"

Fargo would like nothing better, but he lowered the Henry and glided to Tinsdale's side. "Where are you hit? How bad is it?" He caught hold of the older man's shirt. "Let me have a look."

"I'm fine," Tinsdale said, slapping his hand away. "It's just a scratch. Go see about our young friend."

"First things first." Fargo tugged, raising the shirt high enough to verify the bullet had done no more than dig a furrow across Tinsdale's rib cage. The man had been lucky. Another inch to the right and the slug would have torn into his vitals. "You'll live," he said, and headed down the slope.

John was on his back, arms and legs spread-eagle. He had been hit twice, once in the left thigh and again in the chest. "Sorry," he croaked as Fargo examined him. "Things didn't turn out as we wanted."

A sharp retort leaped to the tip of Fargo's tongue. Something about it being the young fool's own fault. But he bit it off and said instead, "The bullet in your leg missed the bone. You'll heal but you'll be limping around for a while." The chest wound was another matter. The slug had ripped through muscle high on his right side, underneath the arm, and exited an inch shy of the right shoulder blade. No organs had been damaged, but John was losing a lot of blood.

"I need to roll you over," Fargo said, and did so. He pried off John's jacket and slid John's shirt as high as it would go to expose the exit hole. "I'll be right back."

"What are you going to do?" John weakly asked.

It was best he didn't know. Fargo ran to the fire and grabbed the unlit end of a thin burning brand. Cupping the flames so the wind wouldn't blow them out, he jogged back and sank onto his knees. "This is going to hurt," he warned.

"What is?"

Fargo jammed the burning brand into the sound. A screech burst from John's throat and he tried to push up off his stomach. Fargo pressed a knee into the small of the younger man's back, pinning him, as the air filled with the stench of fried flesh and burning blood.

"My God! What are you doing to him?" George Tinsdale had come up and was stooped over, an arm to his side. "You'll kill him!"

"Don't think I wouldn't like to," Fargo growled. He held the brand against the wound until the sizzling stopped, until he was positive he had staunched the flow of blood. Then he threw it aside.

John had passed out. Drool seeped from the corner of his mouth and he was breathing unevenly—but he would make it.

"Do you hear that?" Tinsdale suddenly asked.

John's screams and the sizzling flesh had drowned out the thud of approaching hooves. Scooping up his Henry, Fargo dashed to the far side of the gully. It had to be the Swills, returned to finish the job. He reached the lip and brought the Henry to bear. This time he would end it.

Belatedly, Fargo realized the riders were approaching from the south, not the north, and there were more than four riders. A lot more. They appeared around the base of hill, clustered in twos and threes with Simonson and Lafferty at the forefront. Fargo stood and pumped an arm, and at a shout from Simonson, the emigrants streamed toward him. Sweat lathered their horses, and the men were covered with dust.

"So you didn't take my advice either?" Fargo said, frowning.

"We came after Mr. Tinsdale and Carter," Simonson explained.

Lafferty nodded. "That's right. As soon as we found out they had dropped back, we hightailed it after them. We thought we were doing you a favor. We were afraid they would cause trouble for you."

"If you only knew," Fargo said. "My apologies. I'm glad you came." Immensely glad. They could take the pair of nuisances off his hands.

"We were about ready to stop for the night when we heard shots," Lafferty detailed. "We came as fast as we could."

Fargo motioned. "Make camp here. The Swills were kind enough to get a fire going for us. Don't mind the bodies. Just drag them off a ways. The coyotes and buzzards will do the rest."

The emigrants stripped and tethered their animals. Sentries were posted on top of the hill and along the gully. Among the supplies on the pack horses were enough beans to feed a battalion, and soon a huge pot was simmering on a tripod. John and Tinsdale were properly bandaged, and John was carried over near the fire and bundled in blankets.

Tinsdale walked there under his own power and sat sorrowfully staring into the distance. "My sweet Heddy," he repeated every so often.

Badgered by the emigrants, Fargo gave them an account of the gunfight. They were as despondent as Tinsdale at the news that Heddy was still in the Swills' clutches.

"What now?" Simonson asked. "Do we go on after them? Will they kill her or let her live a while yet?"

"I can only answer the first question," Fargo said. "Come first light, you and the others are to take Tinsdale and Carter back to the wagon train. I'm going on alone."

George Tinsdale stirred. "Like hell you are. I'll follow them to the ends of the earth, if need be, without or without your consent."

"It must be my week for jackasses," Fargo said bluntly. He was tired of being bucked at every turn. Tired of having his decisions challenged. "Mister, I've felt sorry for you because Heddy is your daughter. So I let you help out even though I knew it as a mistake." He paused. It was time to let Tinsdale have both barrels. "Well, no more. You and our young friend there almost got her killed. You don't know the first thing about tracking and you're a lousy shot. If you try to follow me tomorrow, I'll shoot your horse out from under you. If you keep following on foot, I'll shoot you in the leg. But get one thing straight. There is no way in hell you're coming along. And that's final."

"Oh, please. You wouldn't shoot me," Tinsdale scoffed. "It would make you no better than those despicable brutes we're after."

"Don't try me," Fargo warned firmly. He would do whatever was necessary to save Heddy. If that required drastic measures, so be it. He had reached the limits of his patience. There was only so much stupidity he would abide.

George Tinsdale was one of those individuals who didn't know when to leave well enough alone. He had set his mind to do something, and he was bound and determined to do it. So Fargo wasn't surprised when Tinsdale shoved to his feet and angrily snapped, "I'm leaving now, before they get too far off. And I dare you to try and stop me!"

"George, please," Lafferty said.

"He won't do it," Tinsdale scoffed. "He thinks he can scare me, but it won't work."

Fargo slowly drew his Colt. He slowly extended it, thumbed back the hammer, took careful aim at Tinsdale's left calf, and when Tinsdale laughed scornfully, he squeezed the trigger.

Shock numbed the emigrants into stunned silence. Tinsdale staggered, then fell. Howling, he gripped his leg and rolled back and forth in a paroxysm of pain. Simonson and several others leaped to his aid.

Fargo stood. The rest had turned bewildered gazes on him. Some appeared ready to go for their guns. Others were utterly dumfounded. "On second thought," he declared, "I'm leaving now, myself. With any luck I'll catch up to your wagon trail in a week to ten days." Twirling the Colt into its holster, he stalked toward the stallion. No one raised a finger to stop him. He climbed on, then kneed the Ovaro over to the fire.

The slug had gone through the fleshy part of George

Tinsdale's calf. The wound was minor, and there was little loss of blood. Tinsdale was livid, but didn't say a word. He had learned his lesson.

"You can thank me when I bring your daughter back," Fargo said. Touching his hat brim, he set out to do what only he could accomplish. He would rescue the man's daughter, or he would die trying.

10

Les Bois lay quiet under the stars. It wasn't quite midnight, but the buildings were dark, the settlement as still as a cemetery. Leaving the Ovaro secreted in a small clearing in the trees where it had grass to graze on, Fargo cat-footed to the rear of the saloon. He had spent twenty of the past twenty-six hours on the trail, stopping at noon for several hours to give the stallion a rest. Although he pushed hard to overtake the Swills, they had good horses and they were able to keep ahead of him.

Half a mile from Les Bois the tracks revealed Clancy and his brothers had swung wide to avoid the settlement, and gone on to the north.

Fargo could either press on after them or give his tired stallion another much-needed break. He chose the latter. Now here he was, sneaking into Les Bois. He would get five or six hours sleep, then head out refreshed.

The back door was bolted from within. Fargo moved around to the side and tried a window. It was latched. He crept to the front corner. The hitch rail was empty. The saloon's customers had long since departed. In a big city like San Francisco or Denver it would be unthinkable. There, drinking establishments stayed open until the wee hours of the morning. But there patrons weren't faced with a long ride over treacherous mountains to get home.

Fargo didn't want anyone to know he was there. Word might reach the Swills, and he wanted them to think they had given their pursuers the slip. When he finally caught up, the element of surprise would be on his side.

Warily stepping to the front door, Fargo confirmed that it, too, was locked. He backed away from the building, he picked up a pebble, and as lightly as possible threw it against Mabel's second floor window. The *plink* it made wasn't loud enough to be heard any distance. Bending, he found another one. But he had no need for it. A faint glow lit the pane, and a second later Mabel pulled the curtains aside. She smiled and waved.

Fargo placed a finger to his lips, then pointed at the front door. Nodding, the redhead disappeared.

Fargo crept to the door and waited. Presently a bolt rasped and the musky fragrance of her perfume tingled his nose. She wore a lacy nightgown that revealed more than it concealed.

"This is a pleasant surprise," Mabel whispered.

"I was hoping to share your bed until morning."

Mabel tittered. "That's not all you want to share, I hope." Snagging his sleeve, she pulled him inside and quietly closed and locked the door. "Lucky for you I wasn't asleep yet. I just got to bed a short while ago."

"Were any of the Swills here tonight?" Fargo inquired.

"Harvey and Leon," Mabel whispered, "the oldest of the bunch. They only stop in every couple of months or so."

Fargo hadn't met them yet. He recollected being told there were nine Swill brothers in all. With Shem and Wilt dead, that left seven, unless the lookout he had slain was also a Swill. Either way, he was greatly outnumbered. "Is Lute Denton still around?" The gambler had struck him as the kind who might be willing to lend a hand.

"Nope. He lit out for San Francisco this morning." Mabel displayed her even white teeth. "He gave me fifty dollars for my special fund, and he never once slept with me. Between him and you, I can leave any time I want now."

"Me?" Fargo said, grinning. "What did I do?"

"I know what you did the other morning. When I

woke up I found the two hundred dollars lying next to me on my bed." Mabel melted against him, her breath warm on his neck. "That was just about the sweetest thing anyone has ever done for me, and I aim to thank you, properlike."

Fargo glanced toward the back room. "What about Barnes?"

"I checked in on him before I opened the front door. He's sleeping like a log. We could whoop and holler and he wouldn't wake up."

"I had something else in mind," Fargo teased. Hooking her elbow, he stepped to the stairs and gave her a playful slap on the fanny. "Ladies first. Just be quiet on your way up."

Giggling, Mabel pranced to her room, her nicely rounded bottom swaying invitingly. "Why all this secrecy?" she whispered as she held her door open for him. "Harry doesn't mind if I have men-friends up. Hell, it's how he earns most of his weekly take. He'll be terribly upset when I tell him I'm leaving for San Francisco at the end of the month."

"That soon?" Fargo stepped to the window and cracked the curtains.

"Why put it off?" Mabel responded. "At long last I have enough money. Frankly, I can't wait to be among civilized folk again. To buy a new dress. To treat myself to a scented bath every day. To dance and drink and have fun." She clasped her hands to her full bosom. "San Francisco will be heaven compared to this flea trap."

Fargo saw no sign that anyone had witnessed his arrival. Removing his hat and gunbelt, he placed them on her table.

"Frankly, I wasn't expecting to ever set eyes on you again, handsome," Mabel said, sitting on the four-poster bed. Her gown parted. Under it she swore absolutely nothing at all. Her upturned nipples, her flat stomach and creamy thighs were enough to make a man's throat go dry.

"Aren't you afraid you'll catch your death of cold?" Fargo said, going over and standing in front of her.

"What I'd like to catch," Mabel bantered, reaching for his belt, "is that redwood of yours." She eagerly unfastened his pants and hitched them down around his knees. After a few more moments, she had his member exposed. "My, oh my," she said, stroking its hardening length. "I believe I'm falling in love."

Laughing, Fargo entwined his fingers in her hair. "Is talking all that mouth of yours is good for?"

"Let's find out."

Fargo stiffened as an incredibly moist sensation enveloped him. Involuntarily, he gasped and pulled her closer. Raw pleasure rippled up his backbone, and he grew iron-hard. He caressed her hair and ran one hand down to the middle of her back.

Mabel was a master. Some women were too rough. Some were too timid. But she had a light, delicate touch, and went about arousing him with an enthusiasm and expertise that was as remarkable as it was enjoyable.

Fargo closed his eyes and let her have her way. The silken feel of her tongue sliding up and down was delicious beyond measure. When she cupped him, lower still, he came close to exploding then and there, but he was able to cap his inner volcano a while yet.

Mabel groaned deep in her throat and one of her hands slid around to the small of his back. Her velvety fingers massaged back and forth and up and down.

Fargo's fatigue evaporated away. He was adrift in sensation, in the feel and smell of her. In due course he eased her onto her back on the quilt. Smiling languidly, Mabel crooked a smooth leg. He feasted on the shapely swell of her satiny thigh and the hint of her charms deeper within.

"You're looking at me like someone who is half-starved for cherry pie and I'm the pie," Mabel joked.

Fargo sculpted his body to hers. She cooed and yielded, her arms rising to encircle his neck. Her breasts cushioned his chest, her hips pillowed his. He kissed her ears, her earlobes, and both sides of her neck. He licked a path from her jaw down across her scented chest to the wonderful swell of her twin melons.

"Oh, my," Mabel said huskily. "You're not the only one who is half-starved!"

Fargo's mouth found her left nipple. At the contact she arched her spine and her hips pumped upward. He tweaked it between his teeth, careful not to nip too hard, then lathered the aureola with his tongue. Mabel's fingers locked in his hair and she panted in rising passion. Covering her other breast with his hand, he kneaded it like a sculptor would knead clay. Before long she was breathing fire on the nape of his neck while her fingers explored his torso.

"You make me wish—" Mabel began, but she stopped and didn't say. Her painted nails scraped his shoulders and dug into his well-muscled arms. "Do me harder," she whispered. "I like it rough sometimes."

Fargo squeezed her right breast, hard, and she groaned loud enough to be heard in Oregon. Her entire body was hot to the touch and she was rubbing her nether mound up and down his leg. Soft, full lips fused to his neck, and her tongue swirled around and around. She hiked at his shirt and soon had it above his shoulders. He shrugged out of it with a flip of his head. Mabel pulled his boots off, then did the same favor with his pants.

Fargo stroked her luxurious hair. He expected her to stand up and embrace him, but she delighted him by planting a series of tiny kisses from his right knee, up across his inner leg, to the junction of his thighs.

By then Mabel's breasts were engorged, her nipples like tacks, and when Fargo pinched one she came six inches up off the bed, her nails digging deep into his biceps.

"Do that again, lover."

Fargo did, and again she reacted in the same way. He kissed her ear and inserted his tongue. It had the effect of making her shiver as if she were cold, when nothing could be further from the truth. Her puckered mouth resembled a pair of burning coals.

It would be nice to spend all night making love, but Fargo had Heddy Tinsdale, Suzanne Maxwell, and who-knew-how-many-other women to think of. At dawn he would ride on. For once he was looking forward to getting done with lovemaking so he could enjoy a few hours of shut-eye.

But Mabel had other ideas. She wasn't in a rush, and when he slid between her legs and went to align his member with her moist core, she gave a little scrunch of her hips that prevented him from coupling until she was good and ready.

Fine, Fargo thought. There were other ways to stoke a woman's furnace. Melding his mouth to a nipple, he slid a hand down over her short, crinkly hairs, to her moist slit. He brushed his middle finger across it and for a moment thought she would buck him clear across the room. Rubbing her engorged knob, he was rewarded with a throaty purr.

"Ohhh, that makes my head swim!"

"What about this?" Fargo plunged his finger into her womanhood. Mabel gasped, then sank her teeth into his right shoulder deep enough to draw blood. He plunged his finger in again and again, settling into a rhythm her hips rose to match. Her left hand found his pole and did to him as he was doing to her.

For the longest while the two of them mutually stimulated each other. A familiar knot formed in Fargo's loins and grew rapidly in size. Her sensual ministrations had him trembling on the brink when he drew his finger out of her wet tunnel, gripped her by the shoulders, and rolled her onto her side so her back was against his chest.

"What are you up to, naughty man?"

In reply, Fargo slid the bulging end of his manhood between her molten thighs. Tensing his hips, he lanced up into her.

"Aaaaaiiiiieeeeeee!" The cry torn from Mabel's throat rose to the ceiling, and she arched herself against him. "Yes! *Yes!*"

Reaching around in front of her, Fargo cupped both swollen globes. He kneaded them while pounding into her, each upward thrust of his hips enough to lift her a few inches off the quilt. Meanwhile, his mouth lathered her neck and shoulders. They rocked in unison, two bodies pumping as one.

The room filled with their heavy breathing, punctuated intermittently by Mabel's soft mews.

"Oh! Oh! I could do this forever!"

So could Fargo. He was in complete control now. Maybe it was fifteen minutes later, maybe it was twenty, when his throat grew parched and his groin twitched, sure signs of imminent release. He was able to hold off a while yet, long enough to reach down and stroke Mabel where it would have the most effect.

"*Ahhh!*" Mabel shook from head to toe and wriggled her bottom in fevered excitement. "I'm almost there!"

One more stroke was all it took. Mabel threw back her head and let out with the loudest groan yet as her body erupted in a paroxysm of release. He felt her inner walls contract around his manhood. And that brought on his own explosion. He lanced into her, nearly driving her up off the bed, and at each thrust she shuddered and moaned. Under them the four-poster bed bumped and shook as if in the grip of an earthquake.

Fargo reached the pinnacle, and held her close. Together they gradually coasted down from the summit of pure ecstasy back to the sweat-caked here-and-now. Together they lay sucking in deep breaths while tiny stabs of delight pulsed through them.

"You do things to me no other man ever has," Mabel breathed.

Fargo returned the praise with some of his own. "You have great tits."

Mabel laughed and rubbed herself against him. "Another thing I like about you is how much fun you are. Most men have the sense of humor of a tree stump."

"You don't say," Fargo said, and gave her bottom a pinch.

Yelping in mock pain, Mabel disengaged herself and turned around so they were face to face and chest to chest. She rested her cheek on his shoulder and toyed with a strand of his hair. "You haven't said what brought you back here? Was it me?"

Careful how he answered, Fargo said, "You're enough to tempt any man, but I'm after the Swills. They've been abducting women from wagon trains. No telling how many, but someone has to put a stop to it."

Mabel raised her head. "Abducting women? Are you serious? I've always thought those miserable so-and-so's weren't worth a pile of outhouse fertilizer. I want to hear all the details."

Fargo left nothing out. After he finished, he inquired, "How far is it to their homestead?"

"I wouldn't know, handsome," Mabel said. "I've never been into the Seven Devils Mountains. Nor has anyone else that I know of. The Swills aren't exactly the friendliest folks around. Except for when they come in to drink or buy supplies, they keep pretty much to themselves. And they've made it plain they don't cotton to unwanted visitors."

That stood to reason, Fargo mused, since they wouldn't want anyone to talk to the women they abducted.

"But now that I think about it, I have wondered about a few things," Mabel remarked. "Unlike the other settlers, the Swills never talk about their wives. You would almost think they didn't have any women out there, but Ziegler, over to the general store, says the Swills buy ladies' things from time to time."

"No one ever thought to question them?"

"The Swills? They don't like people who pry into their business. Mr. Ziegler asked Clancy once how old Clancy's wife was, and Clancy pistol-whipped him into the dirt. Told Ziegler it was none of his damn business and he'd better keep his nose out of Swill affairs."

The store owner's offer to hire Fargo to kill the Swills now made a lot more sense.

"That's not all," Mabel said. "Most settlers bring their wives to the settlement fairly regular. But not the Swills. Never once in all the months I've been here have they ever brought their women in. I always thought it was damned peculiar, but I wasn't about to say anything and have my head split open."

Fargo rolled onto his back and laced his hands behind

his head. He had his work cut out for him. The Seven Devils Mountains were as rugged and inhospitable as any on the continent. But maybe, just maybe, locating the Swills wouldn't be as difficult as he might suppose. They made frequent trips into Les Bois so there must be a trail leading right to their doorstep. Which prompted a question. "Do the Swills live together, do you know?"

"From what I've gathered they have their own little community up there," Mabel revealed. "Each with his own place. Even that snot-nosed brat, Billy. Their ma died back in Arkansas, but their pa is still alive. Pushing eighty, I hear. I've never seen him, either."

A thought occurred to Fargo that hadn't earlier—one that could complicate things. "Do any of the Swills have kids?"

"Not that anyone knows of," Mabel said. "That, too, always struck me as strange. They all have wives but no sprouts?" She giggled. "You know how curious us females can be. I had to bite my tongue at times to keep from snooping. Good thing I did. I don't mind admitting those Swills scare the living hell out of me."

Fargo closed his eyes and willed himself to relax. He needed sleep, needed it badly, but for long minutes it wouldn't come. His mind raced. He couldn't stop thinking about the missing women and what he might find back in the Seven Devils. Mabel fell asleep nestled on his chest, and he listened to her rhythmic breathing until it lulled him into dreamland. His slumber was thankfully undisturbed, and he awakened at the crack of dawn, reasonably refreshed and raring to go.

No sooner did Fargo swing his legs over the side of the bed than Mabel stirred and propped herself up on one elbow, her eyes mere slits. "You're fixing to leave already, handsome? Barnes never needs me until noon. Why not stick around?"

"I can't," Fargo said. Not that he wouldn't have liked to. Pecking her cheek, he swiftly dressed, donned his gunbelt and hat, and walked back over to the bed. "Thanks again for everything."

"You've got that backwards, big man. I'm the one who

should be thanking you." Mabel pulled him down and passionately glued her lips to his. She let her mouth linger, her hands roaming over this chest, until Fargo broke the kiss and stepped back.

"I really must go."

Mabel sighed and lowered her cheek to the quilt. "I must be losing my touch. There was a time when there wasn't a man alive who could resist my charms."

"Your charms are as potent as ever," Fargo said. "But lives are at stake."

"Say no more. After what you told me last night, I can't wait for the Swills to reap the whirlwind. Those poor gals! I wonder how many are still alive? If any?"

There was Fargo's main worry in a nutshell. The women might all be dead. It would explain what the Swills were doing with women's jewelry. Then again, it could simply be that the Swills didn't let their captives keep personal effects. He paused in the doorway. "Next time I make it to San Francisco, I'll look you up."

Mabel grinned. "Don't you dare! By then I'll have hooked a well-to-do gentleman for my husband, and I don't want anyone to raise his suspicions about what I did before he met me."

"Fair enough," Fargo said, smiling. He quietly descended the stairs and went out the back door. The sun was rising as he entered the woods and gathered up the stallion's reins. He rode northward, and once past the settlement searched for the well-worn trail he was sure would be there. It was, sure enough, and for the next half an hour Fargo held the Ovaro to a trot.

Then the trail branched. The right fork bore straight into the heart of the Salmon River Range. The left fork led toward the Seven Devils Mountains where the Swill clan had their lair.

No one knew exactly how the Seven Devils Mountains had earned their name. Old-timers claimed it had something to do with an ancient Indian legend about mysterious hairy giants the Indians battled at the dawn of time. Such legends were common but whites rarely put any stock in them.

Fargo had no idea how far he had to travel. Mabel was of the opinion the Swills lived fifteen or twenty miles from the settlement, but Harry Barnes once mentioned to her it was more like fifty or sixty.

The morning came and went and still Fargo saw no trace of habitation. The trail came to a ford across the Payette River, and once on the other side it pointed him toward the high southernmost peaks of the Seven Devils range. Peaks, interestingly enough, bordered by the Snake River to the west, and not all that far, as the crow flew, from the Oregon Trail.

Fargo stopped for half an hour shortly after noon, then pushed on. The trail climbed gradually but steadily. By the middle of the afternoon he was miles into the Devils range and still had no sign of where the Swills dwelled. He passed through meadows of buttercup and columbine. He crossed valleys choked with elderberry. He rode through woodland tracts of lodgepole pines, ponderosa pines, red cedar, and spruce. And still the trail ushered him ever onward, ever higher.

No other whites called the Seven Devils Mountains home. The range was too remote for even the most reclusive of backwoodsmen. But not the Swills, oddly enough. It made Fargo suspect they had *deliberately* picked the Seven Devils. They wanted more than privacy. They wanted to ensure no one ever disturbed them. They had something to hide, something no one from the outside world had suspected—until now.

A bright gleam of sunlight ahead brought Fargo to an abrupt stop.

The trail wound between rocky spires hemmed by impossibly steep slopes. It was a pass into the next valley, and dozens of feet up on the left-hand spire was a lookout. The man had just shifted position, and thanks to a flash of sunlight off of his rifle, Fargo spotted him before it was too late.

Reining the Ovaro into cover, Fargo slid the Henry from its scabbard, tied the reins to a low limb, and stalked forward until he could see the lookout clearly. If it was a Swill, it was one he hadn't met; a man in his forties or so, with a bushy beard and a floppy hat. Seated in a notch in the rock, the lookout was puffing on a corncob pipe. How he got up there, Fargo couldn't say.

The man appeared bored. Since it was unlikely the Swills posted sentries day in and day out, Fargo imagined that Clancy Swill had taken the precaution because Clancy suspected he would track them down.

Fargo stepped to a log and made himself comfortable. He cold afford to be patient. He had found their hide-away, and they weren't going anywhere any time soon. Should they try, they had to make it past him.

Picking the lookout off would be child's play, but Fargo wasn't inclined to announce his arrival. The man kept squinting up at the sun as if anxious for it to set.

The afternoon waned. The lookout got his wish and the sun fled the sky for another twelve hours. Twilight spread across the Seven Devils Mountains. From the far side of the pass came a loud clanging. The lookout rose, smiling happily, and hastened out of sight around the spire.

The instant the man was gone, Fargo rose and jogged toward the pass. He wanted a look before the last of the light faded. He left the Ovaro where it was. Stealth was called for, and as he neared the towering spires, he slowed.

The lookout was nowhere on the spire or the adjoining slope.

Fargo moved into the pass. Too late, he heard the scrape of leather soles on rocks. Too late, he turned and spied the lookout descending a narrow footpath bordering the left-hand spire, a path that hadn't been visible from the trail until he was right on top of it. Fargo tried to backpedal, to get out of there before the man saw him, but the very next moment the lookout glanced up.

"What the hell! Where did you come from?"

"I'm a prospector," Fargo said, hoping it would gain him the seconds he needed to get close enough to resort to the Arkansas toothpick. Smiling, he moved forward. "My horse threw me and I've been wandering through these mountains half the day."

"You don't look like no prospector to me," the man

said. He had halted and was suspiciously fingering his rifle.

"Why? Because I don't carry a pick around with me?" Fargo stalled. Another few steps and he would be within springing distance. "If you want, I can show you some of the nuggets I've found."

"You know what I think?" the lookout said. "I think you're lying through your teeth." And at that, he started to raise his rifle.

11

Skye Fargo reached the lookout in a single bound and slammed the Henry's barrel against the man's rifle. He hoped to knock it out of the lookout's hands, but he only partly succeeded.

The man's grip slipped and his rifle tilted toward the ground. Springing back, he sought to bring it level again.

Fargo was on him in a twinkling. This time he drove the Henry's barrel into the pit of the man's gut and the lookout folded like an accordion. Again Fargo swung, smashing the Henry's stock against the man's head.

The lookout pitched onto his face and was still.

Fargo glanced beyond the spires to see if anyone had witnessed their clash, but he need not have worried. The trail entered heavy woodland and meandered out of sight down into a lushly forested valley. No cabins were visible but he did spot tendrils of smoke.

Squatting, Fargo set the Henry down, grabbed the lookout under the arms, and hoisted him over a shoulder. It took some doing. The man weighed upward of two hundred pounds.

Holding a rifle in either hand, Fargo slowly straightened and hurried back down the trail to the Ovaro. Nearby was a tree trunk. Propping the lookout against it, he retrieved his rope and securely bound the man to the bole.

Next, Fargo removed the lookout's boots. The odor that rose from the man's filthy socks was almost enough to make him gag. He stripped the right sock off and put it aside. Then he gave the lookout a few light slaps.

The man sucked in a deep breath and mumbled a few words, but didn't revive. He had a small scar on his left cheek, and judging by the grime on his neck, it had been ages since he'd taken a bath. At the next slap his dark eyes opened and he blurted, "What the hell?" Then he saw Fargo. "You! Who are you, mister, and what do you want?"

Palming the Colt, Fargo pressed the muzzle to the lookout's cheek. "I'll ask the questions. You're one of the Swills, aren't you?" He was fishing for information. Gossip had it several close friends, like Porter and Gib, lived in the same general area.

"I'm Harvey Swill," the man said proudly. "The oldest of us boys."

"How many more are on the other side?" Fargo nodded at the pass.

Harvey looked him up and down. "I ain't about to say. Kill me if you want, but now that I've had a good gander, I know who you are. You're that fella who has been giving my brothers so much trouble. The one who killed Shem and Wilt and Donny."

"Donny?" Fargo repeated, and remembered the lookout he had stabbed. So it had been another Swill, after all.

"Play innocent, but it won't work," Harvey spat. "You can cut me into bits and I still won't say."

Fargo had nothing to lose by asking anyway. "Is Heddy Tinsdale still alive? Or Suzanne Maxwell? Or any of the other women you and your brothers have abducted?"

Harvey's lips curled in a sneer. "So you know about them, do you? But you're not as smart as you think you are, not if you came here by your lonesome. My kin will turn you into wolf bait without half trying."

To keep the man talking, Fargo commented, "You didn't really think you would get way with stealing women, did you?"

"Why not?" Harvey countered. "We've been doing it for pretty near three years now and no one else ever caught on. Now each of us has our own gal. The notion worked just like our pa said it would."

"Your father came up with the idea?"

"Pa is the canniest coon alive," Harvey bragged. "We needed females and there weren't any to be had hereabouts. So we did what the Swills have always done. We took what we wanted." He chuckled. "Ten women to do the chores and cook and keep us warm at night."

"Ten? I thought there were only nine of you," Fargo said.

Harvey's eyebrows curved in amusement. "Pa needed one, too, didn't he? We got his gal first since it was his brainstorm, and he's getting on in years."

Fargo hadn't reckoned on so many. Spiriting five or six out of there would be a challenge. Getting ten out safely might be more than he could accomplish alone, but he had to try. "Why didn't you just bring women with you from Tennessee?" he asked as he picked up the sock he'd tossed aside earlier.

"None of the local girls to home would have us," Harvey said indignantly. "They claimed we were no-accounts and fought shy of us wherever we went. So we packed up and came West."

"Open your mouth wide."

Harvey did no such thing. "What are you fixing to do with that thing? Gag me? Not on your life, mister. I'll bite your damn fingers off."

Fargo shrugged. "If that's how you feel about it," he said, and slugged the man in the stomach. Predictably, Harvey bellowed in pain, and with the speed of a striking hawk Fargo shoved the balled up sock into his wide-open mouth.

Harvey sputtered and coughed and tears welled in his eyes.

"They say that washing your clothes once a year doesn't hurt," Fargo remarked as he drew the Arkansas toothpick. Smoothly, methodically, he cut a long strip from Harvey's shirt and tied it tight around Harvey's mouth to keep him from spitting the sock out. "I'd breathe through my nose if I were you," he advised.

Taking the Henry, Fargo returned to the spires, padded on through the narrow pass, and followed the trail down into the hidden valley. High trees hemmed him on either side. The twilight was deepening and it wouldn't be long before night fell. He heard the clanging noise again. It sounded a lot like the metal triangles ranchers used to call in the cowhands at meal time.

A bend loomed. Fargo heard faint voices, and a sound that could have been the slamming of a door.

Past the bend, the trail dipped sharply to the valley floor. Watered by a gurgling stream, the Swills' haven was a mile long and half a mile wide. Hundreds of trees had been cleared north of the stream, the timber used in the building of ten cabins. Each Swill had his own. They were arranged in a large circle that encompassed acres, and in the center, taking up a whole acre itself, was a communal corral.

Fargo counted twenty horses, four mules, and, of all things, a pair of oxen. Some of the horses he recognized; Clancy's, for one—Gus's for another. The women were nowhere to be seen. Nor were any children out and about. But he did spot a pair of Swills on the far side of the corral. Gus was fiddling with a saddle while Billy talked up a storm.

Ducking into the trees, Fargo worked lower. He was particularly alert for dogs, but saw none. On nimble feet he crept through the tall pines until he was an arrow's flight from the nearest cabin. Some of the cabins were lit up, but not this one. Its windows were as dark as the encroaching night.

More and more stars speckled the vault of sky. A door to a cabin across the way opened and Clancy Swill stepped out. "Gus! Billy! Any sign of Harvey yet?"

"Not yet," Billy responded. "Maybe he didn't hear."

"Or maybe he's asleep again," Clancy groused. "The two of you go fetch him. And if he's dozed off, give the lazy cuss a solid kick in the britches while you're at it."

"Will do," Gus said, and poked his younger brother

with an elbow. Together they tramped around the corral toward the trail.

Fargo lay flat. He could drop both of them with ridiculous ease, but it would forewarn the rest. He saw Clancy go back inside.

"I don't see why we're going to so much bother," Billy groused as they crossed to the trail. "We gave those stupid pilgrims the slip. They're not about to track us this far."

"Maybe so. But if Pa says we take turns standing guard, then we take turns standing guard whether we like it or not." Gus scratched under his armpit. "Besides, another couple of days and we won't have to."

"True enough. If those emigrants haven't shown up by then, they never will," Billy stated.

"It's not the tenderfeet who worry me," Gus said. "It's that damned scout. I saw him on top of that hill. He's the one who led the ambush, I'm sure of it."

"He doesn't scare me none," Billy said. "Sure, he put lead into me once. But next time I won't give him the chance. I'll back-shoot the buzzard."

"Not if I do it first," Gus said. "I think he's one of those *pistoleros* we hear tell about. They're chained lightning on the draw, and they hardly ever miss. Back-shooting is the only surefire way to kill 'em."

Fargo let them go by. It had become so dark that within moments they were lost in the gloom. Their footsteps dwindled. Rising, he stalked to the nearest cabin. Like the others, it had two windows, one at the front, another at the side. His back to the wall, he quickly stepped to the side window. The burlap curtains had been left open but he couldn't make out a thing. It was like looking into a well.

Sidling to the front, Fargo crouched and crabbed to the door. Gingerly, he tried the latch. It rasped, and he pushed the door wide. A rank odor assailed him, but nothing else. Darting inside, he shut the door behind him and crouched to wait for his eyes to adjust.

The place was a pig sty. Dust covered everything. Greasy pans and dishes were piled on a counter next to a rusty basin filled with dirty water that stank like the south end of a northbound buffalo. There was a rocking chair and a small rug that had seen better days. Over against the opposite wall was a rickety bed with no sheets and a single frayed blanket.

No one was there. Fargo figured it must belong to one of the dead Swills, or maybe to Harvey, and he turned to go. Suddenly a noise brought him around, cocking the Henry as he did. It had sounded like the clink of steel on steel. And it came from a door in a far corner.

Fargo hadn't realized the cabin had two rooms. Overall, it wasn't all that big. Edging across, he heard the *clink* again. He put his ear to the wood and thought he detected an intake of breath. Then, gripping the latch, he lifted and extended the Henry.

A tiny whine fluttered from the throat of a frail figure huddled on the filth-ridden floor of a small closet. The figure raised its spindly arms over its face to protect itself, and the source of the *clinking* was revealed in all its stark horror. A short chain linked the figure's ankle to the closet wall.

"Damn them," Fargo said softly.

It was a woman. A young woman who must have been lovely once, but now was reduced to a wretched shadow of her former self. She was skin and bones, her dress, or what little was left of it, hung in tatters. Her hair was a tangled mess, her face and most of her body was streaked with grime. Wide, terror-struck eyes regarded him much as a fawn would regard a mountain lion.

Fargo reached out to touch her, but she recoiled as if he were a grizzly. "I'm here to help you," he said. "I'm not one of them."

The woman stared dumbly, uncomprehending.

"I want to take you out of here," Fargo elaborated. "You, and all the other women being held captive." He bent toward the chain and again she recoiled and whimpered in abject fear. "Please, ma'am. I can't do it without your help."

The women blinked and slowly lowered her arms. "Ma'am?" she said in a tiny, quavering voice.

"My name is Fargo," he introduced himself. "What might your name be?"

"Suzanne," the young woman revealed. "Suzanne Maxwell."

Fargo was speechless. *This* was the Carter girl? Jack's and John's sister? The blushing newlywed who had only been missing for three months? The Swills had reduced her to the level of a starved animal. "Your brothers asked for my help—" he began, and was completely unprepared for how she reacted.

Suzanne Maxwell heaved up out of the closet and tried to throw her broomstick arms around him in heartfelt relief. But the chain was too short. She was jerked back and crashed against the wall. Dazed, she melted to her knees.

Fargo knelt and took her into his arms. She felt unnaturally light. Her hair, her body, her dress, gave off a foul odor that was enough to turn his stomach. "How could they do this to you?" He was appalled. Didn't the Swills care that their women reeked to high heaven? What manner of men were they?

"Punishment," Suzanne Maxwell said. "I won't do as Shem Swill wants. I'm his, you see. And until I give in, he won't let me bathe or go outside or put on clean clothes."

"Shem is dead," Fargo informed her.

Suzanne looked up, her eyes filling with tears of profound happiness. "He's dead? Are you sure?" She clutched at him, her bony fingers tugging pitiably at his shirt. "Are you honest-to-God sure?"

"I should be. I'm the one who shot him."

"You?" Suzanne slumped against him and began to bawl in great racking sobs. The fact that the Swills had been unable to break her showed she was an extremely strong-willed young woman. But now that her tormentor was gone, she could no longer contain her emotions. The only thing was, she had to.

Fargo covered her mouth with his hand and whispered into her ear, "We can't make noise or the Swills will hear us."

Suzanne had more grit than most men. Sniffling and dabbing at her eyes, she nodded and stemmed the flow. "I'm sorry. It's just that after all I've been through, you can't imagine how glad you have made me."

"I have some idea," Fargo said. Leaning down, he inspected the chain. It was attached to her ankle by a thin metal band fitted with a lock. "Where does Shem keep the key?"

"He carries it with him, I think."

Fargo knew better. He had gone through Shem's pockets and there hadn't been a key in any of them. Rising, he roved the room, searching through drawers, in cabinets, anywhere a person normally kept a key. He couldn't find it and was about to give up and try to bust the chain when the dull glint of metal on a thin peg to the right of the closet caught his eye.

The moment the lock opened, Suzanne pushed to her feet. In her eagerness to escape she failed to take into account her weakened state. She took one step and her legs caved in under her.

Fargo caught her and braced her with his left arm. "Take it slow," he cautioned. The Henry in his other hand, he moved toward the door. "I'll hide you off in the trees, then I'll come back."

Suzanne grew paler than she already was. "I don't want you to leave me! Please! If they catch me, they'll kill me. It's one of their rules. Any woman who tries to escape is staked out and skinned alive. I saw them do it once."

"I don't have any choice," Fargo said. "There are the other women to think of. I'm not leaving until all of them are freed."

"All ten?" Suzanne said. "Well, with my brothers' help maybe you can pull it off."

"Jack and John aren't with me." Fargo refrained from telling her about Jack's death for the moment. She had been through enough.

"You're alone?" Suzanne's anxiety climbed. "Listen to me. You need help. You can't do it by yourself. There are too many of them."

Fargo opened the door a fraction, enough to scour the corral and the clearing. Holding on to Suzanne, he hurried around to the side and on into the woods. Twenty-five yards from the cabin he gently deposited her in high weeds that would screen her from prying eyes. "Don't move. Don't make a sound." He patted her shoulder and turned to go.

"Mr. Fargo?" The terror had resurfaced, and Suzanne Maxwell was a frightened little girl once again.

"Ma'am?"

"Don't let them kill you. I couldn't stand it if they dragged me back. I will kill myself before I let any of those beasts have their way with me."

Fargo smiled and squeezed her hand, then jogged back to the clearing. Shem and Billy hadn't returned yet. Six of the cabins were lit up now. Since Shem's wasn't and Shem was dead, he reasoned that the other dark cabins must belong to Wilt, Donny, and Harvey. And they all might harbor a captive, just like Shem's.

To reach the next dark one Fargo had to pass two others. He stuck to the treeline, and as he came close to the second lit cabin he heard the front door open. A tall man walked a dozen yards out into the rectangle of light that spilled through the doorway and surveyed the valley from end to end.

Fargo stopped in his tracks.

The tall man stretched and admired the stars a bit, then strolled back inside. All he had been doing was getting a bit of fresh air.

The curtains covering the side window of the next dark cabin had been pulled shut. In a crouch, Fargo worked his way to the front window, but it was the same. Hoping he wasn't making a mistake and those inside weren't asleep, he poked his head in.

This cabin was cleaner than the first, but not by much. A pot was on the stove, and the fragrance of soup or stew filled the room. In the center sat a table, and in one of the chairs facing the door was a vague shape whose waist-length hair left no doubt she was a woman. She was slumped forward, her hair over her face.

Entering stealthily, Fargo shut the door behind him.

To his astonishment the woman snapped to her feet and stood at attention as if she were a raw recruit in the military.

"I'm sorry I dozed off, master! It won't ever happen again! I was tired, was all, and Heddy—" The woman stopped in confusion. "Wait a minute. You're not Leon. Who are you and what do you want?"

Fargo straightened and moved toward her. "I'm not one of the Swills. I'm here to help you escape this place."

The woman was older than Suzanne Maxwell by a good many years. Her homespun dress was plain but adequate. She was clean and her hair had recently been brushed. "Escape?" she said uncertainly. "We're not allowed to escape. My master has made that clear. It's one of the rules. He's beaten me many times for trying, and I don't want to be beaten ever again."

"What's your name?" Fargo had to convince her to go with him before Leon Swill showed up.

"Geraldine Moore," the woman said. She wasn't chained as Suzanne had been. Her arms and legs were free and she could leave whenever she wanted.

"How long have you been here, Geraldine?"

"I can't rightly say. Years, I think. I've lost all track of time." Geraldine nervously swiped at a stray bang. "But I shouldn't be talking to you like this, mister. It's against the rules for us to speak to strangers. My master wouldn't like it."

Fargo's resentment of the Swills intensified. This woman had been cowed into submission, her spirit crushed, her will bent to theirs. "Geraldine, there's no need for you to stay here any longer if you don't want to. How would you like to see your family again? You must have relatives somewhere?"

"My master is my only family," Geraldine intoned. "The Swills are my only relatives. Anyone who says differently is a liar."

Fargo had the impression she was reciting by rote sentiments that had been pounded into her. "Look at me, Geraldine." He smiled to prove how friendly he was. "I'm no liar. I can get you to safety if you'll let me."

139

"My master is my only family," Geraldine reaffirmed. She was about to say more but suddenly she pressed a hand to her temple and winced as if she were in pain. "Oh! What is happening to me? My heard hurts. I can hardly think."

By then Fargo was beside her. Taking her elbow, he suggested, "Why don't I take you out of here? You'll feel a lot better once we're outside."

"My master is—" Geraldine bleated, but she was unable to finish. She staggered, righted herself, and groped at him for support. "I don't know what to do, mister. Part of me wants to go with you, but I'm afraid. Godawful afraid."

"I won't let any harm come to you," Fargo vowed. But keeping the promise might pose a problem, especially if the Swills caught them together. Clasping her hand, he moved to the front door. Suddenly he stopped. Someone was approaching the cabin, whistling as he came.

"My master!" Geraldine blurted, aghast.

Spinning, Fargo propelled her into the chair she had occupied. "Don't let on I'm here!" he whispered, and darted over to stand behind the door. He had barely done so before the latch grated and the door was pushed open within inches of his face. Boots tromped on the rough-hewn planks and a gravelly voice rumbled.

"I trust you've got my supper ready! 'Cause if you don't, I'll tar you within an inch of your life."

Geraldine offered no reply.

"What the matter with you, you dumb bitch? Cat got your tongue?"

Fargo peeked out. The thunderstruck woman was staring right at his hiding place. Her lips were moving, but no words came out. Confronting her was a granite slab with shoulders as broad as a bull's and enough muscle to lift the cabin. Leon Swill was a veritable brute who looked like he could tangle with ten bobcats and come out unscratched.

"Well?" Leon goaded. "Say something, damn your hide, or I'll get out my club and teach you how to behave around your betters." He pushed the door shut without looking behind him, then took a ponderous step toward her.

Wishing Geraldine would stop staring, Fargo elevated the Henry to bash Leon Swill over the back of the head.

But the more bestial the man, the more bestial his senses. Leon Swill was no exception. Something warned him, a sixth sense common to predators and predatory men alike. Whirling, he uttered a feral roar and charged.

Fargo had no chance to dodge aside. It felt like a ten-ton boulder had slammed into him. He was lifted clear off the floor and smashed against the wall. Pinpoints of light danced before his eyes and he lost his grip on the Henry. Fingers as thick as railroad spikes bit deep into his neck. With a supreme effort of will, Fargo collected his wits and stared into the contorted animal features of the hulking slab of sinew who was striving to throttle the life out of him.

"Die!" Leon Swill hissed.

Fargo pried at the man-brute's fingers to no avail. He swung a fist that glanced off a jaw made of iron. He drove his knee at Swill's groin, but connected with more muscle. Struggling fiercely, he glimpsed Geraldine Moore. She was rooted to her chair, paralyzed by fright, and would be of no help whatsoever.

"Die!" Leon roared again.

Twisting and thrashing, Fargo fought for his life. He punched. He kicked. But it had no more effect than if he were beating on a tree stump. His breath was choked off and his lungs were fit to burst. He swung his whole body to the right, then to the left. Nothing worked.

"Die!"

Fargo was close to blacking out. In desperation he made the fingers of his right hand as rigid as ramrods and speared them into Leon Swill's eyes. Not once, not twice, but three times, and at the last blow Swill howled and let go.

Stumbling backward, Leon furiously blinked his eyes, trying to clear his vision.

Fargo kicked him between the legs. He had to slow

the mountain of muscle down long enough to grab hold of the toothpick. Gunshots would bring the others.

Leon was made of solid stone. The kick didn't phase him. But he was still blinking. He still couldn't see clearly.

Quickly, Fargo bent at the knees to grab his toothpick. A painful jab in his spine disabused him of the notion. Pivoting, he stared into the muzzle of a cocked Prescott single-action Navy revolver, and then past it, into the glittering eyes of the revolver's owner.

"We meet again," Clancy Swill said.

12

Skye Fargo clawed his way up out of a bottomless pitch-black pit into the light. He became aware of sounds around him, of a man's cough and the rattle of pots and pans. He smelled coffee and eggs and tobacco. He also experienced an excruciating stab of pain in the back of his head.

Fargo's memory of who caused the pain returned in a rush. It had been the previous night. He had turned to find Clancy Swill holding a gun on him, and behind Clancy, two others. The tall man he had seen stargazing earlier, and a wizened scarecrow who looked old enough to have fought in the Revolutionary War. He had slowly raised his hands. To do otherwise invited certain death.

"I've got to admit, mister," Clancy commented, "sneaking in here like this proves you have more grit than most. No brains, but a lot of grit."

"We do what we have to," Fargo answered.

"Ain't it the truth. And guess what my brothers and me have to do to you now that we've caught you?" Clancy was going to say more, but his eyes widened and he bawled, "No, Leon! Don't!"

That was when the cabin's roof came crashing down onto Fargo's skull and he was smashed to the floor with bone-jarring force. Hard, steely fingers clamped around his throat again, and the world grew dark.

Now, opening his eyes, Fargo took stock. His head was pounding. His wrists were bound, but not his legs. He was lying on his side on a cabin floor but it wasn't Leon's cabin. This one was clean and tidy. Sunlight streamed in through a side window decorated with flowery curtains. A brunette was puttering around over at a stove. He twisted his head to see the rest of the room and a low groan escaped him.

"Well, well," Clancy Swill declared. "Look who decided to rejoin the land of the living? You've been out all night and most of the morning." Clancy was seated at a table adorned with a yellow table cloth. Beside him sat the elderly man with more wrinkles than a prune. "You're lucky to be alive, mister. Usually when Leon wallops someone like he walloped you, they never get back up again."

"Brother Leon is as strong as a bull," agreed someone outside of Fargo's line of vision.

"If Pa hadn't stopped him, he'd have stomped your noggin as flat as a flapjack," remarked a third party, and everyone laughed.

Fargo slowly swiveled around. Gus and Billy Swill occupied chairs over by the wall. Hunkered near the front door was yet another—Harvey Swill.

"That's right," Gus crowed. "We found Harvey and cut him loose. We brought your pinto along, too. Didn't want it getting lonesome."

Billy tittered. "That's a mighty fine animal you've got there, Mr. high-and-mighty scout. I reckon I'll keep it for myself."

Fargo tried to speak, but his throat was as dry as a desert. He had to wet his mouth and swallow a few times before he could croak, "Why—?"

"Why are you still alive?" Clancy finished for him. "Why didn't I let Leon finish you off?" He winked at the old man. "Tell him how things are, Pa."

The patriarch of the Swill clan shifted in his chair and coolly regarded Fargo with eyes amazingly bright and alert for someone his age. Bright, alert, and sinister, for there lurked in them a suggestion of vicious intelligence and latent cruelty. "So you're the polecat responsible for the deaths of three of my boys? You're the cur who's dogged them clear across the territory?"

Fargo didn't dignify the question with an answer.

"I'm Jericho Swill," the patriarch announced. "Blood kin means everything to me. My boys are my pride and joy, and I don't take kindly to having them rubbed out." He thrust a gnarled finger at Fargo. "The only reason I had Leon spare you is so we can kill you proper. You need to pay, but you need to suffer first. Before we're through, you'll beg us to end your life. I guarantee."

Fargo had heard similar threats before; from the Blackfeet, from the Apaches, from the lowest outlaws and the most vile cutthroats. Ignoring the Swills, he studied the woman. She perplexed him. She was humming cheerfully, as if she didn't have a care in the world.

Clancy Swill was observant. "You look surprised, Fargo. You figured all the gals we stole would be like that first one you set free. The Maxwell girl. Well, they ain't. Once they've been with us long enough, they get used to it."

The woman glanced at him and smiled, but Fargo noticed that the smile didn't touch her eyes.

Clancy was still talking. "Where *is* the Maxwell woman, anyhow? We've looked all over and can't find her anywhere."

Dread knifed into Fargo. In Suzanne's condition she wouldn't last long on her own. Had he rescued her from their clutches only to doom her to perish of starvation or thirst?

Jericho Swill rose stiffly and shambled around the table. "When my son asks you a question, you miserable son of a bitch, you'd best answer him." Snapping his right leg back, he delivered a savage kick.

Agony exploded in Fargo's ribs. He doubled, bile rising in his throat, and had to resist an urge to slam his legs into Jericho's. It would only bring on the wrath of the others.

The patriarch and his sons cackled lustily. Then Jericho moved toward the door, saying, "Bring him. It's time we got started."

Clancy and Gus seized Fargo by the arms and hauled him out into the glare of the late morning sun.

Jericho's cabin was on the north side of the clearing. He stepped to a metal triangle suspended from a post, removed the small slim bar that hung from it, and began striking the triangle again and again. Loud peals echoed across the valley. He continued to strike it as cabin door after cabin door opened.

Fargo saw Leon striding toward them like a great, riled bear. He saw the tall Swill whose name he hadn't learned yet. And with them came Geraldine and the rest of the women. It was a gathering of the clan.

Jericho stopped banging on the triangle and turned to those assembled. "Brethren!" he shouted, raising his hands over his head. "The moment we have been waiting for has arrived! The moment when we exact our vengeance for the lives of Shem, Wilt, and Donny!"

Fargo wondered how they intended to do it. Would they stake him out and skin him alive, as Suzanne had said they were fond of doing? Or did they have an equally hideous fate in mind?

"All of you know me," Jericho Swill said. "All of you know I'm a fair man. I never harm anyone unjustly. The Good Book says we should give as we receive. An eye for an eye, a tooth for a tooth. But what do we do when the crime is so foul? How do we make this man pay for the loss of three of our loved ones?"

"Let's rip his innards out, Pa!" Leon Swill bellowed.

"We could do that, yes, son," Jericho said, nodding, "but he'd die awful quick, wouldn't he? Is that fair, I ask you? Is that just retribution for the dearly departed?" His wrinkled mask of a face clouded. "I say no! I say he must suffer! I say he must be made to grovel for mercy. Then, and only then, will his sorrow compare to ours."

"What do you have in mind, Pa?" Harvey asked.

"I propose we kill him a bit at a time," Jericho said. "We'll whittle him down like a block of wood, piece by piece, until there's next to nothing left. Then, and only then, will we send him to hell where he belongs."

Leon rubbed his hands together in sadistic anticipation. "How do we start, Pa? Do we cut off his fingers and toes?"

"All in due time," Jericho said, grinning. "We'll wait until he's hungry enough to eat them." The old man gestured at Clancy and Gus. "Do as we talked about, boys, and be quick about it."

Fargo was half-carried, half-dragged to a spot midway between the cabin and the corral. He was thrown to the ground, and Leon and Harvey came over to hold his legs. Billy drew a pistol and pointed it at his face. Gus untied his wrists.

Clancy ran back into the cabin and reappeared with a hammer, four wooden stakes, four lengths of rope, and something else, the sight of which made Fargo grit his teeth in expectation of what was to come. "What are you waiting for, Gus?" he demanded.

Gus Swill stripped off Fargo's shirt and threw it to one of the women. Then Gus grabbed one wrist, the tall Swill grabbed another, and Leon and Harvey seized Fargo's feet. None-too-gently, they flipped Fargo onto his stomach and his limbs were stretched so he was spread-eagle in the dirt. "We're ready," Gus said.

Clancy sank onto a knee beside Fargo's right wrist and pounded a stake into the earth. When it was deep enough to suit him, he tied Fargo's wrist to it, gave the rope a few tugs to ensure it would hold, and moved around to Fargo's other wrist.

Fargo was helpless to resist. Not with four men holding him down and Billy Swill holding a pistol on him.

Harvey pulled off the left boot and tossed it away. Leon wrapped his huge fingers around the right boot, and wrenched.

"Well, lookee here, Pa."

They had discovered the Arkansas toothpick. Leon unfastened the sheath and threw it to his father, who examined the knife and remarked, "Nasty things, these pigstickers. When the time comes, we'll use it to chop off his fingers and toes." He passed the toothpick to Gus.

Soon Fargo was tied fast, and the Swills stepped back to admire their handiwork. "He ain't going anywhere." Harvey grinned.

Jericho was holding the last object Clancy had brought

out. Now he gave it a practiced flick and the tip cracked as loud as a gunshot. "Know what this is, son-killer?"

Everyone on the frontier had seen a bullwhip at one time or another. Fargo clenched his teeth and steeled himself for the ordeal to come.

"You have an annoying habit of not answering questions," the patriarch said. "What say we break you of it?"

The bullwhip cracked, searing Fargo with pain that nearly took his breath away. His right shoulder felt as if it had been split to the bone, and a damp sensation spread down his back.

The Swills chortled, Leon loudest of all. "Do it again, Pa!" But none of the women, not even the merry brunette, shared in the glee.

"Happy to oblige, son," Jericho Swill said, and swung the bullwhip again.

Fargo remembered being told it wasn't the first strike of a whip that hurt the most. Nor the fifth or the tenth. It was the twentieth and thirtieth, when a person's back had been cut to ribbons and their swollen flesh was so tender that each blow was enough to make them go insane with agony. But he begged to differ. The next several swings of the lash sliced into him like sabers, and it was all he could do to keep from crying out.

Unexpectedly, Jericho stopped and began coiling the whip.

"What are you doing, Pa?" Leon asked. "Keep it up until he looks like chopped meat."

"Weren't you listening, son?" Jericho replied. "A piece at a time, remember? We'll let him lie there a while, then do it again. And again. And again. And again. Until he's groveling at our feet."

"Don't hold your breath," Fargo said, and was treated to another kick in the ribs.

"We'll cure you of sassing us," Jericho promised. "This time tomorrow you'll lick our boots clean if we tell you to, and be glad to do it." He walked toward his cabin. "Right now everyone else is invited in for sweetcakes my woman baked."

Amid much laughter and boisterous chatter, the Swills and their captive women filed indoors. A few of the women cast sympathetic glances at Fargo, but they were careful not to be seen doing it. He didn't blame them. If caught, they would be beaten, or worse. He lay quietly for a few minutes, listening to the nicker of a horse in the corral and the caw of a raven high in the sky. His back was a welter of pain.

Merriment issued from the cabin. The Swills were having a grand old time.

Fargo strained against the ropes binding his wrists, but couldn't budge them. He tried to move his legs with a similar result. He was completely at the mercy of men who had no mercy. They could do with him as they pleased and there wasn't a damn thing he could do about it. Closing his eyes, he prepared himself mentally for the next whipping. He refused to show weakness, refused to give his tormentors the perverse pleasure of hearing him cry out.

The Swills left him alone for a long time, an hour or more. Then the door opened and out they marched, reeking strongly of alcohol. Gus was carrying the bullwhip, and he gave it a few swings to limber up.

"I trust you weren't lonely, mister," Jericho mocked him. "We would have been back out sooner, but we were placing bets on how long you'll last."

"I give you three days," Gus Swill said. "No one has ever lasted that long, but you're one tough hombre." His pudgy arm rose and fell.

Fargo thought he would bite off his tongue. The pain was infinitely worse. It tore through him like a burning brand through soft wax. And it was only the first of ten or eleven Gus delivered. By the end Fargo was half-conscious and as limp as a wet rag. He was grateful when the blows stopped, so grateful he almost thanked Gus aloud, almost thanked the buzzard who had put him through it.

"Time for more food and drink!" Jericho Swill declared. "Everyone into my cabin and we'll pass around another bottle."

Pounding waves of anguish pulsed through Fargo. Blood was dripping from his sides and soaking the top of his pants. He barely had the energy to raise his head and watch the Swills go in. As soon as the door closed he gathered his remaining strength and violently twisted his wrists back and forth. He had to free himself. Another couple of whippings and he would be too weak to make the attempt.

The rope bit deep into his skin. Fargo resisted the discomfort and kept twisting, twisting, twisting. He lost track of time. His shoulders ached but he didn't stop. His wrists were pools of agony but he didn't give up. The rope grew slick with blood, and he was able to move his wrists a little. Encouraged, he twisted harder.

Suddenly the door opened. Fargo feigned unconsciousness as the Swills gathered around for another go at him.

"He's passed out on us, Pa!" Billy declared. "Let's wait a while. It's no fun when we can't hear 'em squeal."

"Hold your britches on, boy," the patriarch said. "Harvey, wake our guest up. We don't want him to miss out on the festivities."

Fargo lay still as the oldest son clomped into the cabin. Soon Harvey was back. His footsteps came closer, ever closer, and the next moment Fargo was deluged with a bucket of water. He swallowed as much as he could, and felt brief, soothing relief spread across his back and down his arms. Licking drops from his face, he grinned at Jericho Swill. "Thanks. I needed that."

Jericho wasn't amused. His face flushing, he motioned at Billy, whose turn it was with the bullwhip. "He think's he clever, boy. Show him what we think of his cleverness."

Billy Swill took to the task with unrestrained zeal, cackling with each swing. The deeper the lash bit, the louder he laughed.

Gritting his teeth, his fists clenched and his shoulders bunched, Fargo endured the onslaught in stoic silence. It angered Billy, who soon stopped cackling and applied the bullwhip with redoubled vigor.

"Scream, damn you!" *Crack.* "Why won't you do like

the rest?" *Crack.* "What makes you so different?" *Crack.* "Scream! Or so help me I'll whip you until you do!" *Crack.*

Fargo girded for yet another blow, but it never came.

Jericho Swill had grabbed his youngest son's wrist and was wresting the whip from Billy's fingers. "Enough, boy! How many times must I repeat myself? We want him to die nice and slow. Keep cutting into him like that and you're liable to put him out of his misery much too soon."

Billy cursed, but he let go. "I've never hated anyone in my life as much as I do this varmint, Pa," he snarled. "I can't wait to bury him."

"Patience, boy. All things come to him who has the patience to wait for them." Jericho squinted at the sky. "We'll let him lie there until sundown, then start in again fresh. Everyone might as well go on about their business until then."

Fargo was left alone. Closing his eyes, he laid his cheek in the dirt. The pain was almost too much to bear. To complicate matters, fatigue gnawed at him. Not from lack of sleep but from the brutal flogging. He craved rest but he didn't dare doze off. He would just lie there a moment, then work on freeing his wrists. Just a minute. Or maybe two. That was all he needed to pull himself together.

With a start, Fargo opened his eyes and lifted his head. Shadow mired the valley, and the air was considerably cooler than it had been. He had slept the afternoon away! A sliver of sun was all that was left. Soon it would be gone, and the Swills would resume torturing him.

"No," Fargo groaned aloud, and tried to twist his right wrist. It was abominably stiff and tremendously sore, and moving it required every ounce of will he possessed. He turned to his other wrist.

For a moment Fargo couldn't believe his eyes.

Suzanne Maxwell was crawling toward him. Half-starved though she was, bedraggled and filthy and as weak as a kitten, she clawed at the earth to pull herself along. A few more yards and she would reach him. And wonder of wonders, in her left hand she held a butcher knife.

Fear gripped Fargo. Not fear for his sake. Fear for hers. The Swills would kill her if they caught her. He glanced at the patriarch's cabin, then scanned the clearing. No one was outdoors. It was the supper hour, judging by the mouth-watering aromas borne on the breeze, and everyone was indoors eating. But for how much longer?

Suzanne painstakingly pulled herself another couple of feet nearer. The determination on her face was a thing to behold. Every muscle, every line, was stretched taut. Her jaw was carved from marble, and her eyes gleamed with an inner light.

Fargo's mouth went dry. He could scarcely stand the suspense. She had to reach him. *She had to.* Again she laboriously dragged herself along. Only four feet to go now. "Hurry," he whispered, every nerve jangling.

Suzanne's response was a fierce grin and one last heave. She slumped against his arm, exhausted, and whispered, "I wondered what was keeping you."

Her courage, her humor, her sacrifice on his behalf, brought a lump to Fargo's throat. "They'll be outside any minute," he warned.

Grimly, Suzanne sawed at the rope. But she was so weak she could hardly wield the butcher knife. Refusing to admit defeat, she gripped the hilt with both thin hands and slashed at the loop. Her first stroke sliced a third of the strands. Her next completed the job. "There." She looked at him in silent entreaty, and collapsed.

Heedless of how much it hurt, Fargo grabbed the knife, rotated at the waist, and cut his other hand free. His back screamed in protest as he bent and made short work of the restraints binding his ankles.

A sudden swell of newfound energy coursed through him. Rising, Fargo strode toward Jericho Swill's cabin. The window glowed with light. He didn't know how many were in there and he didn't care. He walked right up to the door, wrenched on the latch, and shoved.

Jericho was at the table, spooning stew into his mouth.

The woman in the yellow dress was in a chair on the other side of the room, knitting.

Shock rooted them in place as Fargo stalked toward the table. The patriarch dropped his spoon, shoved upright, and turned toward a pair of rifles propped against the wall. He never reach them. Two swift strides brought Fargo close enough to streak the blade across Swill's throat.

A scarlet geyser spurted. Jericho flung his gnarled hands to his ruptured jugular and tried to shout but couldn't. Tottering wildly, he clutched at the table, missed, and sprawled in a convulsing heap.

Fargo glanced at the woman. He thought she would scream, but all she did was nod a few times, then go back to her knitting as if nothing out of the ordinary had occurred. He looked at the rifles again. One was an old flintlock. The other was his Henry. And near them, hanging from a peg, was his gunbelt.

Dropping the knife, Fargo strapped the Colt around his waist. He picked up the Henry and worked the lever to feed a round into the chamber. Outside, someone was shouting. He turned to leave, and caught a glimpse of his reflection in a mirror. He almost didn't recognize himself. His back was crisscrossed with angry welts and vicious cuts. Dried blood caked his shoulders and chest. In his bare feet, and with his hair disheveled, he looked like a wild man from the remote depths of the woods.

"Pa! Pa! Come a running! That Fargo fella has escaped!"

Without a pause, Fargo walked on out.

Billy Swill had been doing all the yelling. "You!" he exclaimed, and flashed a hand for his revolver.

Fargo already had the Henry to his shoulder. He fired as Billy drew, fired as Billy tried to take aim, fired as Billy's legs caved, and as he did a slow pirouette to the earth.

Doors were opening all around the circle and Swills were rushing out with weapons in their hand. A rifle spat lead. A pistol banged twice off to the right.

Lead sizzled the air as Fargo fed a new round into the

153

Henry and advanced. The tall Swill whose name he had never learned was firing at him from the corner of a cabin. He snapped a shot, and when the tall man tottered forward, mortally stricken, he fired twice more for good measure.

Around the corral rushed Harvey Swill. He paused to take precise aim and in doing so made it that much easier for Fargo to drill a .44 slug through the center of his forehead.

Fargo shifted to the right. Gus had burst from another cabin and was charging toward him, holding a shotgun. They fired simultaneously. Gus rushed his shot and fired high, but Fargo's round split the heavyset's Swill's head like a sledge cleaving a rotten melon. Gus Swill toppled like a fallen tree.

More gunfire blasted.

Clancy Swill was at the south end of the corral. He had climbed to the top rail and was firing from the hip.

Fargo filled the Henry's sights with Clancy's silhouette. He pulled the trigger, pumped the lever, then stroked the trigger again. He saw Clancy jerk once, jerk twice, and keel off the rail.

Quiet fell. Fargo slowly lowered his rifle. He tried to remember how many he had disposed of, and who might be left. A reminder came in the form of a pair of enormous arms that swooped around him from behind, pinning his own arms to his sides. Suddenly he was in the grip of a human vise.

"I'll kill you!" Leon Swill ranted. "Kill you, kill you, kill you!"

Fargo let go of the Henry and flicked his hand to his Colt. It cleared leather as Leon lifted him off the ground and shook him like a bear shaking a badger. Bending his wrist, Fargo jammed the Colt's muzzle against the man-mountain's groin, thumbed back the hammer, and fired. Leon howled and his grip slackened. Enough for Fargo to wrench partway around and jam the barrel into Leon's left eye. "Kill this," he said, and fired.

For long moments afterward Fargo stood breathing deep of the crisp night air. At last it was over, truly over.

They were all dead. Or were they? He heard footsteps and whirled, but it was only several women. They stopped, too timid to come nearer.

"Are you all right, mister?" one asked.

Fargo slid the Colt into his holster. His back was throbbing and his legs had grown weak. "I could use some help, ladies."

They came to him, then, and supported him as Fargo moved toward the bedraggled figure by the stakes. "She saved me," he said, and knelt to turn Suzanne Maxwell over. Her head lolled against his leg. Gripping her wrist, he felt for a pulse, and when the truth dawned, he threw back his head and shook the stars with his rage. *"Nooooooo!"*

The three woman pressed back in fear.

"Are you sure you're all right, mister?" asked the same one as before.

Skye Fargo looked up, his eyes glistening in the lantern light. "No," he said softly. Cradling Suzanne Maxwell in his lap, he bowed his head. "I may never be all right again."

THE TRAILSMAN #248
Six-gun Justice

*Northern California, 1860—
The lust for gold brings the
death of honor, and the muzzle
of a gun brings the birth of justice.*

An eagle wheeled through the sky far overhead, and
Skye Fargo reined the Ovaro to a halt to watch. His
lake-blue eyes shone with his appreciation of the scene's
beauty. Not only the eagle, this northern California landscape itself was one of the prettiest things Fargo had
ever witnessed. The highest, snow-capped peaks of the
Sierra Nevadas loomed over smaller mountains whose
slopes were covered with thick, blue-green forests of pine
and cedar and spruce. Fast-running, sparkling creeks
twisted through the valleys. Over all of it was the blue
vault of the sky, dotted here and there with puffy white

clouds. Fargo thumbed back his hat and smiled. He patted the sleek black shoulder of the big paint horse. Up here in the high country, it was hard to tell that Man had ever touched this land.

Then Fargo stiffened as gunshots began to blast in the distance.

He should have known better than to start thinking about how pristine and untouched this land was. He knew good and well that a little over a dozen years earlier, thousands of men had flooded into northern California, drawn by the lure of gold. Ever since James Marshall had noticed something shining in the waters of the creek beside Sutter's Mill, nothing had been the same here.

Fargo listened to the shots, his keen ears picking up the sounds of at least three different weapons. From the way the reports were spaced, he could tell that one person was fighting back against several. He had ridden into the Sierra Nevadas just a couple of days earlier, so he had no idea who was shooting at each other, but he knew he didn't like the odds. He heeled the Ovaro into motion and headed down the slope of the hill on which he had paused.

There was a road at the bottom of the hill. Fargo turned to the north and urged the horse into a faster gait, just short of a gallop. He didn't want to ride blindly into what was sure to be a dangerous setting. As he drew closer to the sound of shooting, he eased the Colt in its holster on his right hip, then drew the Henry rifle from the sheath attached to his saddle.

The road took a sharp turn and plunged down to cross a creek at the bottom of a little draw. A wooden bridge spanned the creek, or at least, it would have if someone had not come along and chopped holes in the timbers. At the side of the road just short of the bridge, a buggy with a black canopy lay on its side. The wheel that was on the top side of the overturned buggy was still spinning. One of the mules hitched to the buggy was down, motionless and probably dead. The other was still in its harness.

Fargo surveyed the scene as he pulled the Ovaro to a stop. He saw puffs of gunsmoke coming from behind a cluster of rocks on the creek bank, not far from the ruined bridge. Whoever had been in the wrecked buggy must have taken refuge there. More shots came from the trees along the slope to Fargo's right. Those would be the bushwhackers, Fargo decided.

To his eyes, the story told by what he saw was clear as day. The bushwhackers had chopped holes in the bridge, then opened fire on the buggy as it started down the hill. The buggy's driver hadn't seen the ruined bridge until it was too late to stop without wrecking the vehicle. He must have been thrown clear in the crash, and he had scurried into the rocks, forting up there to put up a fight.

Even without knowing the driver of the buggy, Fargo was certain whose side he was on in this fight. He swung a buckskin-clad leg over the Ovaro's back and dropped to the ground.

Holding the Henry slanted across his chest, Fargo moved into the trees. Rifles cracked and pistols barked as the bushwhackers continued to pour lead down at their intended victim. From the bottom of the slope, a heavier roar sounded as the man in the rocks fought back. He was using an old percussion pistol, Fargo judged, and the gun wouldn't be very effective against the sort of odds he faced.

Fargo was going to do what he could to even those odds.

He spotted a man crouched behind a tree, firing a pistol down toward the creek. Fargo stopped and took aim, then squeezed the trigger of the Henry. The rifle bucked against his shoulder. He saw the bushwhacker's hat fly into the air and heard the startled yelp that the man let out. Then Fargo was on the move again, darting behind the thick trunk of a tall pine.

He crouched and used the underbrush for cover as he worked his way along the slope. The man whose hat he had shot off yelled, "Hey! There's somebody else up here!"

Fargo bellied down onto the ground as he located another of the bushwhackers. The man was between a couple of rocks. From this angle, Fargo didn't have a clean shot at him. But there was more than one way to skin a catamount.

Fargo snugged the butt of the Henry against his shoulder and began to fire as fast as he could work the rifle's lever. The slugs smashed into one of the rocks that hid the second bushwhacker and ricocheted into the space between the boulders. The gunman howled in surprise and fear, and the narrow part of his body that Fargo could see disappeared from view as the man hunted better cover.

Something crashed through the brush behind Fargo. He rolled over and reached down with his right hand to palm the Colt from its holster. He saw a flicker of black and white through a gap in the brush and recognized it as a cowhide vest. Fargo triggered two quick shots in that direction, then rolled again and came up on his feet. He darted behind a tree as bullets smacked into the trunk, sending slivers of bark flying into the air.

"Who is that son of a bitch?" one of the bushwhackers shouted.

"I don't know! I never got a good look at him!"

Fargo holstered the Colt and went to hands and knees to crawl along the slope. He came to a sharp drop-off and slid down it, landing in some fallen pine boughs at the bottom. He worked back toward the road a short distance, then picked up a broken branch and flung it through the air so that it made a racket in the undergrowth to his left. When the bushwhackers fired toward the sound, Fargo sent three fast shots screaming through the trees around them.

"There's more than one of them! Damn it, I'm gettin' out of here."

He heard more sounds of men struggling through the

thick undergrowth. If he had wanted to, tracking them would have been no trouble. But he was content to let the three men go. He had spoiled their ambush without being forced to kill anyone, and rescuing the driver of the wrecked buggy was all he had set out to do.

Fargo waited until he heard hoofbeats receding in the distance. Then he waited some more, just to make sure the bushwhackers weren't trying some sort of trick. When he was satisfied they were really gone, he walked back to the road and whistled for the Ovaro. The horse came trotting down the hill to him.

Fargo slid the Henry into its sheath and took hold of the Ovaro's reins. As he led the horse down the hill, he called, "Hey! You in the rocks! Those gunmen are gone!"

The percussion pistol boomed, and Fargo came to a sudden stop as a heavy slug kicked up dirt in the road about twenty feet ahead of him. "Don't you come no closer, dadgum it!" an elderly man's voice shouted from the rocks on the creek bank. "How do I know you ain't one o' the varmints your ownself?"

Fargo stayed where he was, not wanting to tempt a trigger-happy old-timer into shooting at him again. He kept his hands in plain sight and said, "I'm the one who ran them off. Didn't you hear me shooting at them?"

"I heard a bunch o' shootin', but you can't tell which side a gun's on by listenin' to it."

He had a point there, Fargo admitted to himself. "All right, I can't prove it. But if I was one of the men who were trying to kill you, would I be standing out here in the open like this?"

"Maybe, if you was a tricky enough bastard."

"All right," Fargo called. "Reckon I can just mount up and ride away and leave you here. But you'll have a hell of a time getting that buggy back on its wheels by yourself." He turned away from the creek, gathered up the Ovaro's reins, and put a foot in the stirrup, ready to swing up into the saddle.

"Wait just a dadblasted minute!" the old-timer shouted from the rocks. "There ain't no need to be so damned touchy!"

Fargo took his foot out of the stirrup and waited. A moment later, a man in a dusty black suit and hat emerged from the rocks on the creek bank. Long white hair fell almost to his shoulders, and a bristly white beard covered his jutting chin. He held an old Dragoon Colt in his right hand and used the weapon to wave Fargo closer.

Leading the Ovaro, Fargo walked on down to the ruined bridge. The old man made his way along the creek bank and met Fargo there. Rheumy eyes studied Fargo's muscular six-foot frame and ruggedly handsome features. The old-timer said, "You don't look like no bushwhacker I ever seen."

"That's because I'm not. Name's Skye Fargo."

The old man grunted in surprise. "The Trailsman?"

"That's right."

"I heard of you. You're supposed to be able to track a grain o' sand through a duststorm."

Fargo laughed. "I wouldn't go so far as to say that."

"Never heard anything about Skye Fargo bein' a dirty damned back-shootin' killer, though, so I reckon I can trust you." The old-timer stuck out his hand. "I'm Judge Jameson Boothe, ridin' the circuit from Sacramento."

Fargo had decided already that the old man was either a judge or a preacher. That explained the sober black suit, the white shirt, and the black string tie. Boothe didn't talk much like a judge, but Fargo knew that out here on the frontier, jurists weren't exactly like their counterparts back east. It was a rugged land, and rugged men were needed to settle it. Even a smattering of legal knowledge often qualified a man to be a judge west of the Mississippi.

Fargo shook hands with Boothe, then said, "Looks to me like somebody was trying to stop you from getting to where you're going."

"That's the double-damned truth of it, son. I started ol' Damon and Pythias down the hill, and them hydrophobia skunks opened up on me from the brush. I lit out and never noticed until I was nearly at the bottom that they'd chopped holes in the bridge. That buggy o' mine was gonna wreck one way or the other." Boothe looked at the dead mule and sighed. "Almost wish they'd ventilated me instead o' poor ol' Pythias. He was a damned fine mule."

Fargo commiserated in silence for a moment over Boothe's loss, then said, "Where are you bound, Judge?"

"Headed for a settlement called Ophir. Ever heard of it?"

Fargo frowned in thought. "The name sounds familiar. Wasn't it a boomtown back during the Gold Rush?"

"Sure was. Some o' those Forty-Niners took a heap o' gold dust and nuggets out of there. Then the color sort of played out for a long time. Now there's rumors floatin' around that a big strike's been made up there, and folks are flockin' in again. You know what that means?"

Fargo nodded. He knew, all right. All it took was a hint that gold had been found, or was about to be found, and men hungry for wealth would descend on a place from all over. And not only prospectors and miners, but also all the hangers-on who came with them: gamblers, saloon owners, soiled doves, bullies, gunmen, killers who would murder a man in the blink of an eye. The dregs of civilization. Most of the miners were honest, upstanding men, even though temporarily blinded by their lust for gold. But those who followed them from camp to camp, boomtown to boomtown, were anything but honest and upstanding.

"The decent citizens of Ophir sent word of their troubles to Sacramento," Judge Boothe went on. "They asked the state for help, and I reckon I'm the answer."

"You'll have a big job on your hands," Fargo said. "There'll be a certain element in the settlement that won't want any sort of law and order established."

"You ain't tellin' me nothin' I don't already know, son. I reckon that's why them scurvy bastards've tried to kill me more'n once since I left Sacramento."

Fargo frowned. "This ambush today wasn't the first time someone's tried to kill you?"

"Nope. I managed to outrun 'em twice before." Boothe gave a regretful laugh. "Them mules o' mine can run faster than anybody would think they could, just by lookin' at 'em. I reckon that's why the skunks decided to get in front of me and set up an ambush this time."

Fargo nodded in agreement. "Makes sense, all right. What are you going to do now, Judge?"

"Why, go on to Ophir, of course! I ain't never shirked my judicial responsibilities before, and I'll be damned for a lowdown polecat if I start now!"

Fargo gestured toward the bridge. "We can get your buggy upright, but it won't make it across there. And the creek's too deep and fast for you to ford it."

Boothe tugged at his beard and frowned in thought. After a moment, he said, "I reckon you're right. I'll have to unhitch Damon and ride to town on him."

"How much father is it to Ophir?"

"I figured to get there 'round noon tomorrow."

Fargo glanced up at the sky. There wasn't more than an hour or two of daylight left. Riding the mule might turn out to be slower than using it to pull the buggy. Mules were balky creatures, and most of them didn't like to be ridden. Still, in all likelihood Boothe could reach Ophir before dark the next day, even riding the mule.

"Someone can come out from the settlement and repair the bridge, then bring the buggy on into town," Fargo said. "Why don't you get anything you need out of it while I unhitch the mule?"

Boothe squinted at Fargo and asked, "Are you plannin' on ridin' with me to Ophir, son?"

Fargo grinned. "I was heading in that general direction anyway, and I don't have any place else I have to be. That's one of the advantages of drifting."

"Hmmph. That ain't much of a life for a grown man to be leadin'. I ain't complainin', mind you. I'll be glad for the company, especially if them bushwhackers show up again."

Fargo didn't say anything, but the same possibility had crossed his mind. If someone had tried three times to stop Judge Boothe from reaching Ophir, a fourth attempt wasn't out of the question. And he knew that was why he had come to the decision he had. He felt an instinctive liking for the feisty little jurist, and he didn't want to see any harm come to him.

Less than half an hour later, Fargo led the Ovaro across the bridge, the horse placing its hooves so as to avoid the holes. Boothe followed, tugging on the reins he had fashioned out of the mule's halter. "Come on, you jughead," Boothe urged the mule. "I don't like leavin' Phythias here, neither, but we ain't got no choice."

When they had crossed the bridge, Fargo gave Boothe a boost onto the mule's back, then swung up into his saddle. Leaving the site of the ambush behind, they rode on through the waning afternoon toward Ophir.